ANN
MAJOR
WILD MIDNIGHT

SILHOUETTE *Desire*

Published by Silhouette Books

America's Publisher of Contemporary Romance

SILHOUETTE BOOKS

ISBN 0-373-05819-5

WILD MIDNIGHT

Copyright © 1993 by Ann Major

This edition published by arrangement with Harlequin Enterprises B. V.

® and TM are trademarks of Harlequin Enterprises B. V., used under
license. Trademarks indicated with ® are registered in the United States
Patent and Trademark Office, the Canadian Trade Marks Office and in
other countries.

Printed in U.S.A.

Prologue

The first time Johnny Midnight, a darkly handsome youth of nineteen, saw skinny Lacy Miller in a swirl of dust and lavender twilight, looking all grown-up, and elegantly slim, he was struck by the rare, heart-stopping quality of her innocence and golden beauty. In the next instant he knew she was in trouble—probably of her own making. Just as he knew he'd probably rescue her anyway.

He had a secret aberration in his hard, street-smart character that flared up at the damnedest times and made him play hero when it would have been smarter to walk away.

But mostly he'd help her because of a not-so-secret yen for beautiful blondes of the creamy-complected, full-bosomed, slender-hipped variety. And she was a masterpiece of that species. One look at her slim, shapely body and he felt hot male needs pulse to life—unexpected, unwanted, but undeniable.

He was in the darkened interior of a rented moving van, straining every muscle in his lean body to shift his mother's favorite one-hundred-pound bureau onto a rented dolly.

Terror stricken, Lacy was flinging herself violently out of Darrell Grumpie's rusted-out car and slamming the door.

It was getting dark, and there was plenty to scare a girl in this neighborhood. Plenty to scare a guy.

Midnight balanced the bureau precariously on one of its flimsy legs, so he could see her better. A year ago when she'd been as straight as a toothpick maybe she could've gotten away with that playsuit, but now her outfit revealed way too much of her sleek honey-toned legs. The white shorts barely covered her adorable rounded bottom. No girl who looked like her should dress so skimpily—not in this neighborhood. Not around guys like him who'd grown up too tough and hard, guys who'd watched friends bleed to death in the filthy gutters, guys who took what they wanted unless someone meaner stopped them.

Midnight's body went so taut in response to her that the cords stood out on his neck—which was unusual because girls around here were too easy to excite him much.

But she was different.

In expensive clothes, she could have passed for one of those glamorous creatures from that other world, the kind who sometimes lounged around the Douglases' pool, half naked in their string bikinis, where he worked his guts out most weekends as the pool boy and gardener. They stirred his hot-blooded ghetto-boy fantasies, but were too good to satisfy them. His knuckles tightened. Dream girls—for a guy like him. The kind of woman he, Midnight, would have—someday. Just as he'd have all the rest—a pool boy and his own gardener.

Even in her simple clothes, she was a California golden girl, and so classy she would have stood out anywhere. But her elegant beauty was all the more vivid against the shabby poverty of the potholed street and narrow, decaying Queen

Anne houses that had been chopped into tenements on the upper stories and into cheap stores or clubs or topless bars on the lower floors.

The only houses that were still single-family dwellings were the house Midnight's family was moving into and its next-door twin. Graffiti had been sprayed on several boarded-up windows across the street. The area had some of the city's worst crimes. But Midnight's father was disabled, and Midnight had just talked Sam Douglas into hiring his father as a night watchman in one of the Douglas warehouses, which was nearby. The cheap rent of this tumbledown house was all they could afford.

The moist air was cool, typical of an early fall evening in San Francisco, and Johnny's lean, muscular body was shirtless.

He'd been shivering in the darkened van, but when Lacy began to walk down the sidewalk toward him, in that quick, light, long-legged gait, he felt his blood heat.

He wondered if she moved like that just to stir up guys like him. Those slim hips that swayed with every step put him into major hormone overload. Major.

But it wasn't just her beauty that drew him. It was the way her wide, silkily lashed eyes darted furtively toward the narrow house next to his; it was the way her vulnerable face got paler with every look.

Darrell gunned the motor, spraying her with smelly exhaust fumes, and sped away.

What the hell was he dumping her off like that for when she was scared?

When a stray piece of garbage blew past her, she jumped skittishly. Then she glanced at her watch, gave a little frantic cry, and scurried across the rough, broken sidewalk toward the moving van, toward him, running blindly like a scared rabbit for the nearest cover.

"Hi there," Midnight murmured, holding the bureau with one hand and grabbing his shirt with the other, and stepping out into the dying sunlight, expecting at the very least a blush or a shy, startled smile because with his tall, dark good looks, girls around here didn't usually take much chasing.

She didn't even look up.

Strike one, lover boy. He shrugged arrogantly and tried to pretend he was too tough and conceited to care.

When the bureau tipped dangerously, he lost his grip on the smooth wood and had to struggle wildly to keep the thing balanced. Then a thin leg snapped, and the bureau crashed down on his heavily booted big toe.

Strike two.

Hot bolts of pain splintered up his shin to his knee.

Stay cool.

Impossible around her. "Damn it! Ouch!"

Midnight didn't usually make such a fuss, but he wanted her to notice him.

She didn't.

He craned his neck so far he got a crick. And no wonder. She had a helluva figure, and she was probably showing it off on purpose just to tease guys like him.

Slim at the waist, big at the top, with every curve jiggling, she had the body of a woman. But she was as light and awkward on her feet as a coltish child, as if her voluptuous body were new to her. A girlish pink bow that tied her silver ponytail bounced as she ran.

Innocence and sensuality—she was a potent combination.

Seventeen, he guessed, remembering she was two or three years behind him in school. Not a day over. Maybe she really was so young, she didn't know what she did to guys like him.

Then a big hand snaked out from the shadowy corner of the porch and grabbed her.

Her helpless wail of terror cut through Midnight as the huge brute slammed her against the wall so hard the house shook.

"No, Daddy! No!"

A nerve in Midnight's cheek began to pulsate as he remembered why guys left her alone—she had a mean old man who was still mad 'cause his wife had run off. The word on the street was that the old bastard would kill anybody who messed with his daughter. Midnight knew firsthand about tyrants, because his own father had gotten bitter and vicious after Nathan's death.

The purple-faced balding guy she called Daddy didn't look much like her. He was as mean and coarse as she was sweet and golden. His hairy potbelly hung sloppily over the gray elastic band of his undershorts which was exposed because his ragged tank top and cutoffs didn't meet in the middle.

Old man Miller chugged the last of his beer, smeared his foamy, thick lips across a greasy forearm and pitched the bottle aside. Then he dragged her ruthlessly inside and banged the door behind them.

Leave it alone!

But Midnight knew what brutes did behind closed doors. In a single jump he bounded out of the truck and raced through the tall grasses of their littered lawn. He leapt up their rickety stairs two at a time, stopping abruptly at their door.

Her pink satin bow, looking torn and fragile, lay in the dirt on the porch. Midnight stooped and brought it to his lips. It smelled of sunshine and roses, of sweetness and innocence—of all the things he'd wanted and never had.

"You're late! Where the hell were you? Who were you out with?" Her father's voice boomed through the thin door.

Her response was small, helpless, lost, dying. She'd played this scene before. "Nobody, Daddy."

"Liar. You're a no-good tramp like your mother. I saw you in the car with him."

"Darrell Grumpie just gave me a ride home from the library. That's all."

"You probably gave him a ride first," her father jeered crudely.

"No, Daddy."

"Then why did he drive away like a bat out of hell?" A fist slammed down hard on a tabletop. "Answer me!"

A chair was hurled against a wall.

Panic tightened Midnight's stomach as he imagined thick-fingered brutal hands on the girl.

Be smart and mind your own business, Midnight. She's probably used to it.

Why did he have to remember a skinny, lost little girl with unkempt braids, standing in the hall at school apart from the other children after her mother ran off—looking as lost and forlorn as he'd felt after Nathan died?

A slap rang out.

She isn't your affair. You don't have to prove anything.

She screamed.

Midnight's fingers crushed the rose satin bow. His long, tautly muscled body jerked forward before he caught himself. His knuckles touched the rough wooden door. Then his fists clenched against the impulse to break it down.

She screamed again.

And he went wild, a crazy killing rage winning out over his hardened ghetto-shrewd mind. He thrust a heavily booted heel forward so fast and so furiously the door splintered.

Lacy sank to the floor, her eyes misting with tears from the blow—a first. Her father had never hit her before, but he was madder than he'd ever been. He didn't like the way boys had started to notice her. The skin on her forehead was stinging and Lacy knew her left eye would puff up and darken, and he'd make her stay home from school a day or two so nobody would know.

Her fingers dug helplessly into the dingy upholstery of her father's armchair as she cowered behind it, her familiar sick terror mushrooming in her stomach—not from her father's raised fist but from the monstrous, drunken hate blazing in his eyes.

The hate had been there ever since her beautiful, gentle mother had run away two years ago. No matter how good Lacy was, and she *was* good, no matter how well she did in school, and she was number one in her sophomore class, her father was never proud of her. He hadn't even come to hear her when she'd sung in the starring role of last year's school play.

Mother, why didn't you take me with you? Every night Lacy's pillow was damp with tears as she cried herself to sleep with that refrain.

Her mother had read her fairy tales about princesses who lived in castles, about maidens who got into terrible trouble and were saved from some hideous fate such as fire-breathing dragons by heroic princes.

Her mother had promised her that some day their prince would come, and they would be saved from their squalid life. Only when their prince had come, her mother had run away with him in the night and left her daughter behind. Her father had blamed Lacy and hated her ever since.

More than anything in the world, Lacy wanted to run away like her mother. But she didn't know a prince, and she was scared of the creeps at school who gave her hot looks and whistled at her and asked her out. Before today she'd told herself that her father had never really hurt her, that she had nowhere better to go, that at least she had her books and her dreams even if her real life was hopeless.

At least it seemed hopeless until Johnny Midnight crashed through her front door like a hero out of one of her books and her father's flying fist stopped just short of her jaw, hanging there like a dying thing before he let it fall.

Father and daughter stared at the incredible dark ghetto prince who loomed intimidatingly in their door, a fierce, killing glare contorting his features.

"Get away from her," Johnny Midnight growled.

Then Johnny looked at her, and the bloodlust went out of his eyes. When his grim mouth gentled, his chiseled face was almost beautiful. And strangely the stinging pain around Lacy's eyes and the nausea in her stomach began to subside.

Her father backed warily away from the young tough.

"You okay, girl?" Johnny's slow drawl was low pitched and velvety when he spoke to her.

Nobody had ever spoken to her like that, warmly, raspily, as if he might care. She looked into Johnny's smoldering black eyes, and the instant she did, his gaze went even softer just as his voice had. And somehow the way his gentleness jarred with his terrifying fierceness sent a shock through her whole body, as if a sweet warm tide of electricity flowed from him to her. His expression stilled as if just looking at her stung him, too.

When he tore his gaze free and strode across the threshold, an angry, brittle tension followed in his wake.

She couldn't take her eyes off *him*. He was the kind of hero her dreams had been made of—tall and dark and fatally handsome. Skintight ragged jeans snugly fit his powerful thighs and long, muscular legs.

He was shirtless, and she gasped at the livid purple scar that zigzagged wickedly across the breadth of his wide bronzed shoulder and then snaked down his gleaming torso. Someone had cut him with a knife.

His beautiful face was bold and dangerously reckless, and his too-knowledgeable brooding gaze made her feel all grown-up and sexy, too, even though she was barely sixteen.

"The name's Johnny Midnight," he drawled unnecessarily in that deep voice, smoothly, politely, almost elegantly, like he was in that fancy drawing room over at the Douglas mansion. At the same time he watched her father in that hard predatory way. "I'm your new neighbor."

"Lacy... Lacy Miller," she said haltingly, liking his roughness as well as the elegance of his manners; liking his smoldering virility.

Midnight grinned. "I know who are you. You sang in our high-school talent show and won first prize."

He'd noticed her.

She knew who he was, too.

Every girl knew.

He'd had a brother who'd died when he was just a kid and a bitter disabled father who drank and went from job to job, always blaming his bosses for his failures and driving his only son to excel. Midnight had been a football star at her school. He'd smiled at her once or twice when she'd been feeling sorry for herself after her mother had run away.

He'd graduated the summer before, and after he had, her school had seemed smaller, emptier. She'd liked watching him swagger down the halls, his black head six inches taller than most of the other guys', with three beautiful girls, fast girls, hanging on him at once. He had a reputation for being smart and fearless and so tough that all the bullies were scared of him. He ran with J. K. Cameron, who was smart and wild and almost as good-looking.

Everybody said the two of them were going somewhere. She'd heard J.K. had gotten a job in the hotel business and Johnny was almost through college now—night school— and that he worked three part-time jobs to earn enough so he could go. She'd heard that he spent his weekends at Sam Douglas's fabulous mansion and took care of the grounds and the pools and the notorious Douglas twins. She knew that because her father worked for Sam Douglas, too, as one of his night watchmen in a nearby warehouse.

Maybe Johnny Midnight had never looked down from the lofty position he held in their rough neighborhood and appreciated her in that hot way before, but as he stared into her eyes with that intense masculine interest, he was rapidly making up for lost time.

He had a dangerous reputation with girls, but even though his eyes were hot, he made her feel special—the way she'd always imagined she'd feel if she were a real princess.

Thus, when he held out a sinewy tanned hand she grabbed it, even though she'd never touched a guy in front of her father. Shivering, she watched in awe as Midnight's long fingers intimately laced themselves through hers. Then the steel-muscled arm shoved her behind him as if, already, she were his to protect.

"You sure you're okay, Slim?" he whispered.

She nodded. Her thick lashes fell against her white cheeks and she stared foolishly down at her sandals.

She felt a callused finger tip her chin. Gently he brushed a tear from her cheek.

His mouth tightening, Johnny turned on her father in a quiet, deadly voice. "If you ever touch her again, if you ever make her cry again, I swear I'll kill you."

"Y-you can't break and enter, punk. This is a family matter. There are laws...."

A muscle convulsed at the corner of Midnight's mouth. "Right." He took a single menacing step.

Her father scrambled toward the phone, but Midnight lunged faster. A fluid brown arm ripped the telephone from the wall and pitched it at her father. Midnight stared Miller down, his black eyes as hard as agates.

Her father slunk against the back wall. "She ain't worth it, kid. She's a tramp—like her mother."

"I'm not," Lacy whispered blindly, tearfully.

Midnight studied her pale face, his strong grip pulling her closer against the hard warmth of his body. "Easy..."

Without thinking she threw her arms around Johnny's waist. *"I'm not,"* she stammered shudderingly.

"I believe you." He smoothed her hair, glaring at her father over her head. "You leave her alone, do you hear me?"

Then, in that velvet baritone that she already loved, Johnny whispered to her, "If he touches you, girl, or even if he just scares you, you tell me. Understand?"

Her eyes darted toward her father and then back to Midnight's sternly carved dark face. She sensed in him the strength, the determination to follow through.

She swallowed hard and nodded.

Yes, she knew who Johnny Midnight was. He wasn't scared of anything. Not even of her father, the way every other boy was, and he would stubbornly defend whatever he believed in. Maybe she should have realized then that that wonderful strength could be a terrible flaw, and that because of it Johnny Midnight would be an especially dangerous breed to cross. But her mind was whirling wildly with crazy new dreams. And this burningly angry and yet strangely gentle ghetto prince was at the center of them all.

Like her mother, Lacy possessed a rash romantic streak that made her believe she could escape the cruelties of her hopeless world.

Her willful face shining, Lacy looked up at Midnight. His dark, compelling gaze caught hers again, and her heart skipped a beat. Instinctively, he drew her closer. Even though she was bewildered by the deep, complex emotions that bound her to him, she smiled up at him shyly, trustingly. She placed a gentle hand upon his warm chest and felt his fiercely thudding heart pumping against her fingertips.

For an instant he seemed both humbled and profoundly uneasy. Then he began to shake almost as violently as she.

His hands gripped her slim waist more tightly. His mouth tightened in an inflexible line.

His strength and determination gave her courage.
She wasn't scared, either—not any more.
Johnny Midnight was going to be her real-life prince.
And he was going to set her free.

One

They said she was the beauty of the century. She was America's most brilliant political wife and hostess, and the story of her charmed life was well known. She'd been poor, orphaned at eighteen, and then rescued by her Prince Charming, the rich and renowned Sam Douglas. She was America's very own Cinderella. The press constantly wrote about her real-life happily ever after.

And when she read about it, it was as if she were reading the story of someone else's life, or rather the fantasy of someone else's life, because it read like one of the fairy tales she'd adored as a child.

How could they know that her life had never been like that at all?

He was a famous older senator. She was his beautiful, much younger showcase wife, the symbol of his much touted virility. But in a way he was as cold to her as her father had been. He was a womanizer. Sometimes he even drank. She'd learned too late that the secretive Douglases were a cold family of twisted passions and obsessive jealousies. Sam had never been her Prince Charming, and she was just a phony princess. Their marriage had been a sham from the beginning.

Torrents of rain drummed against the Douglas mansion in Vienna, Virginia, flattening the thousands of potted tuberoses that Lacy Douglas had had placed along the edges of the wide verandas that afternoon, so that the house would be redolent with their fragrant smell.

In her black velvet sheath and diamonds, Lacy sagged against the massive front door, her exhaustion soul deep as she watched the parade of taillights disappearing down the drive into the gloom.

The last of her rich and famous guests were being whisked away through the dark driving rain in their long chauffeured limousines. She had no way of knowing that an uninvited guest had slipped through the electrified gates as one of the limousines passed through, that even now that black-clad figure was racing across the lawns, stealthily approaching the back of the house.

Lacy's thoughts revolved around herself, and the momentous decision she had recently made about her future and her son's.

Her last party as the fabulous Mrs. Douglas was over.

Tomorrow she would be extolled once again as the perfect hostess, the perfect wife of the famous senator, Sam Douglas. Her exquisite regal posture, her platinum hair, her black designer ball gown, her diamond tiara, her brilliant guests, her perfect house, *her perfect life*—all would be described in richly embellished details. In light of her new decision, that praise would be more ironic than ever.

If the rare reporter noticed that her smile lacked spontaneity, he would say it contained genuine sweetness, generosity, warmth and compassion. If he observed that her expressive violet eyes seemed shadowed by a mysterious sorrow, he would add that their gentle sadness only made her seem more vulnerable. He would go on to say that she was unaffected by her wealth and fame, that she lavished every spare moment on the numerous charities she sponsored, which catered to the needs of poor children.

With a trembling hand, Lacy touched the cold black windowpane, her fingers tracing the sparkling raindrops that raced down the other side of the glass.

It never failed. Dear God.

Rainy nights always made her remember her graduation night and Johnny, and how her life then had been so much more than the colorless existence it was now. That night her heart had throbbed with vital passion and terrible anguish. Johnny, who had had a bitter, loveless relationship with his own impossible father, had been kind after he'd discovered the shameful reason her father hadn't attended her graduation ceremony.

Voices from the past—hers and Johnny's.

Barely past being kids, he was twenty-one and had just finished his first year of law school; she was eighteen. They stood nervously apart, just inside Johnny's tiny room behind the magnificent Douglas pool. Her father had been especially cruel that night, so Johnny had brought her there after the graduation ceremony because she hadn't wanted to go home till her father left for work.

The Douglases, even their redheaded twins, had been out, which Johnny had said was unusual because they rarely went anywhere together. But because they were, he'd boldly shown her the main house as well as the grounds. She'd felt like a princess in a fairy tale wandering through those elegantly lovely rooms with Johnny. She'd written a paper on the senator once, and despite the stories Johnny sometimes told her about the Douglases, she was in awe of them.

After she'd seen the house, Johnny had taken her to his quarters behind the pool. Johnny, who had a fast reputation with other girls, had never been fast with her. Thus, it

was the first time they'd ever even been to his room, and
they were both too aware of the implied intimacy of his un-
made bed.

She lingered at his door in her simple white dress, having
thrown her gown, her mortarboard and tassel as well as her
valedictory medal onto his floor. Johnny's hair was inky
wet, as were the broad shoulders of his dark suit.

The French doors were open so they could hear the rain,
and so they wouldn't be shut in with his bed.

Afraid to look at each other, they'd watched the sparkling raindrops race down the windowpanes.

She peered through the raindrops out onto the sculpture
garden. "This is some house."

"Yeah, but sometimes watching the way the Douglases
cheat on each other and fight, the way the twins get so mad
you think they'll murder each other, and the way the Douglases don't care who they step on to get what they want, I'm
not so sure being rich is all it's cracked up to be."

She touched the windowpane. "Where are the raindrops
going so fast, Johnny?"

"Nowhere special, but they're getting there a hell of a lot
faster than we are, Slim."

"You'll make it."

"Yeah. Someday. Hey—but what if you get tired of
waiting and choose some other guy?"

He shrugged and pretended to smile, but when she saw the
dark strain in his tired face she felt sympathy because he
worked so hard to excel.

"Hey, you're getting wet, valedictorian," he drawled
raspily. "Come away from the door before you ruin your
new dress."

She clung to the door frame, so he joined her there. The
closer he got, the darker the gentle fires blazed in his eyes.
He leaned negligently against the wall. "God, you're beautiful. I was proud of you tonight when you gave that speech.
Your mother—"

Lacy cut him off. "She walked, remember? But who needs her? She brought me up on crazy dreams. She used to tell me Alcatraz was a castle. I remember how awful I felt when Keith Taport bragged his grandfather had done time there. Then you took me, so I could see for myself it was just a prison. So, who cares about her? I've got you now. If you hadn't been there tonight, I would have choked on the first word."

A slow smile spread across his darkly handsome face. "Hey, you can do anything—with or without me, Slim. You don't ever get nervous when you sing."

"Singing comes from the soul."

His hand settled on her shoulder, and she gasped. "Which is the most beautiful part of you," he mused, his low voice devastatingly husky.

"You didn't used to think that."

"I still go for your body, Slim." He tore his eyes from her. But his gaze shot back to her lips.

"Kiss me," she murmured.

When his hot, masculine mouth tenderly nibbled a raindrop off the tip of her nose, her stomach fluttered wildly.
She wanted more.

He shuddered and pulled back. He never pushed for sex because he was afraid that if she got pregnant they'd end up poor and embittered like their parents.

She pulled his tie through his collar and wound it teasingly around her hand. "I mean really kiss me."

He backed away. "We'd better go."

"Why, Johnny?" She ran her fingers along the base of his warm throat, loosening the top button, lingering over the fierce beat of his pulse.

"You know why." His smooth tone belied his raw edginess.

When she touched his hair and stroked his jaw, he stiffened. For two years he'd limited their lovemaking. Who would have believed that tough Johnny Midnight could behave like a gentleman? At first she'd been flattered, but now the frightening hunger he'd aroused never left her.

On a groan he laced his bronzed fingers caressingly through hers. "I didn't bring you here to seduce you."

"I know." He was always so sweet. Maybe that was why she wanted him so much.

"I want more for us—marriage. Someday, Slim—"

But she felt the barely suppressed violence in him beneath the surface, and her own soft sigh was filled with despair. "I want more than someday, Johnny."

"You want a house like this."

"No." She wanted love. *His* love.

"What about your scholarship to college? Hey, I don't want to jeopardize your future."

"Don't you love me?" She brought her hand to her lips and tore her thumbnail loose with her teeth.

Midnight yanked her hand away and ran a fingertip across the rough wounded place. "Hey, will you quit with the self-destructive impulses?"

"No, and I can't wait for someday, either."

He made some smothered oath. Then she touched him through his clothing, and he gasped. His fist knotted. But the sudden warmth that radiated through her when Johnny's savage gaze burned over her made her bolder.

Her hand slid inside his shirt and caressed his bare belly, moving lower until he grew hot and hard and his heartbeat pulsed violently beneath her exploring fingertips. Until he began to pant in an odd, breathless way. Until his skin burned beneath her hand like he had a fever. Until he forgot his stubborn principles and grabbed her and kissed her—roughly, greedily—with fierce lips that made her shivery and breathless, too.

He pulled his lips from hers and sucked in a deep breath. He pushed her away, leaning against the wall, his lean body radiating tension. "If you're smart, you'll leave me alone."

"Why can't we love each other?" No one had ever loved her. Not her mother. Not her father. Only Johnny. Ashamed and scared, she clenched her fists. Surely no decent girl ever felt this hot and achy, never pushed when a guy like Johnny said stop.

Her father's words that he'd shouted earlier that night echoed in her mind.

"I ain't going to see no graduation tonight for the same reason I hate you—because you ain't my kid. The day I found out, your mother snuck off 'cause she knew I'd kill her! She didn't want you, either. Nobody will ever want you—except for one thing. And you'll be easy like her and dish it out to them all, starting with that cheap hood, Johnny Midnight—you probably already have."

No...

The rain beat down, and she threw herself out into the icy downpour, almost welcoming the needle-sharp raindrops that lashed her soft skin, soaking through her dress. She ran toward the pool, welcoming the cold after Johnny's heat. She put her arms around a dripping Doric column, embracing it and laughing hysterically.

Midnight ran after her, grabbing her with rough hands, pulling her back beneath the eaves, folding her protectively against his warmth so she wouldn't shiver.

She felt his pounding heart. The heat of him. His growing stillness. His awareness—of her.

"Crazy, girl. What's with you tonight? God, your dress is almost transparent."

She liked the way his voice rasped. She liked the way his eyes went blacker when he tried not to look at her nipples pushing against the thin wet fabric. She held her breath. He held his too.

Sexual tension bound them together in that damp silvery darkness with the fragile strength of a warmly tangled web. She knew she should struggle against it; she knew she should run, that Johnny would let her. But she couldn't.

"Love me, Johnny. Please, love me—forever." She kissed him again, her trembling wet lips both innocent and bold.

"Forever," he promised hoarsely.

His tongue licked inside the velvety depths of her mouth, and it was as though her body was set aflame. Without another word he pulled her into his room and slammed the door and drew her down onto his bed. His work-roughened hands were all over her smooth, wet skin. Her white dress tore. Not that she cared. She drank in the hot male scent of him, wanting more.

His tongue mated with hers again, fusing his lips to hers with a melting kiss that was deeper and more intimate and more exquisitely exciting than anything she'd ever known, fanning the wild primitive longings that they had both denied too long.

He pushed her dress up, but despite his overwhelming male need, he took time to protect her.

Lightning exploded, but the violent storm that raged behind the sparkling curtain of raindrops racing down the windowpanes was nothing compared to the storm within them.

His pent-up longing was so wild and insatiable, he went too fast. But even that first awkward time was good because his desire for her was so keen and fresh—as if he'd die if he didn't have her. Even so, when she cried out, he stopped and held her until she grew accustomed to his body and kissed him through her tears, begging him to go on. Then he lost all control and held back no longer, and she gloried in the wild, mysterious, shattering joy he found in her body. Afterward, she ached in a funny way, and although she was sore she felt as if she wanted something more, but she lay beside him, clinging, stroking his wet black hair, her whole body tingling and aglow. He said he was sorry and she couldn't imagine why until he made love to her for the second time.

He undressed her slowly, sliding his large hands over her, caressing her breasts. Then his mouth moved lower, over her belly, her navel; lower still until she shyly resisted. Then he wrapped his arms around her and with ardent love words and humble kisses, he persuaded her to change her mind. When his mouth moved between her thighs again, his kisses hotter and more boldly caressing, he seemed to instinctively know all the hidden spots where his lips would arouse her.

Afterward when her hands moved in his hair and brought his darkly flushed face shyly to hers, she knew she was shameless—but she felt too glorious to care.

"Undress me," he ordered in a terse, low tone that was so urgent it excited her all the more.

Shivering and trembling she sat up slowly and clumsily unbuttoned his shirt, sliding it from his muscular shoulders. When she ran her fingertips over his broad chest and flat belly, he sucked in his breath.

"Kiss me—the way I kissed you," he commanded.

His eyes were blazing, and suddenly the strange compulsion to do what he asked came over her. And it was as wonderful as what he'd done to her. *Because she loved him. And he loved her.*

He was trembling with exquisite torment when he moved on top of her, wrapped her closely and sheathed himself again. He was still and gentle for a long moment, savoring the wonder of her. Then she moved her hips, and he began to thrust, his breath coming faster, his passion making her twist and writhe. Until his hands gripped her and he seared his molten lips against her throat, his powerful body jerking convulsively. Caught in the same final vivid white explosion, she arched against him, crying out, his intense pleasure having somehow brought her own.

Afterward they lay together in that shimmering darkness, holding each other. And every time after that that he took her, she'd lost more of her virginal reticence, loving

him more, wanting him more until all the conventional
barriers of modesty and shyness dissolved. He had only to
look at her, to touch her, and instinctively she knew what
sensual gift he wanted from her and how to please him. It
didn't matter any longer that she had never known love before—because she had Johnny.

Nothing in her books, not even her romantic imagination had prepared her for the fiery sensual core of her feminine nature, for the ecstasy of Johnny, who was as intensely
sexual as she was. She truly believed that her excessive sexual pleasure could not be bad if it brought her closer to
Johnny, that her soul had been joined to his as well as her
body, that he loved her, that his love would last forever, that
nothing could come between them.

Later, when they arrived back in their own neighborhood in the early hours of the morning, oddly enough, the
freak storm's only effect had been whipping gusts of wind
rushing down the dark, narrow streets. As Johnny led Lacy
up the steps to her house, they were at first merely curious
about the wicked orange glow that licked the sky above the
area of the warehouse where their fathers both worked.
Even when they heard the sirens and they began to run, they
never really thought the tragedy might involve anyone they
knew.

Shortly after her father had gone on duty, a fire had broken out and roared through Sam Douglas's warehouse,
killing her father and Camella Douglas, who had been dec-
orating the upper story for one of her famous parties.
Johnny's father, who had been terribly burned, died ago-
nizingly months later.

The fire had been set deliberately in three places.

The Douglases swore the arsonist was Johnny's embittered father. When Johnny refused to accept that and hurled
countercharges back at them, Sam Douglas fired him. At
the same time the famous senator kindly opened his home

to the newly orphaned daughter of his other night watchman.

When Lacy moved in with them, Johnny had turned from her. Steadfastly refusing to see any side but his own, he had made her feel abandoned and unloved. Which had made her need the Douglases even more. Thus, he had set in motion the final chain of events that destroyed their love.

Two

Lacy Douglas came back to her unhappy present with a start. The innocent girl who'd believed in princes and heroes, the girl who had surrendered herself irrevocably, body and soul, to Johnny Midnight because she'd thought him kind and gallant, was dead. In her place was a beautiful, glamorous creature, a carefully crafted make-believe princess, who lived what some believed was a perfect life. What for some *would* have been a perfect life. Yet for her, it had been no life at all.

Why did she still blame Johnny now for all that had gone wrong between them—ten years later? She should have known he was too roughly bred to be anybody's knight in shining armor. Why did she blame him for shutting her out when she'd needed him most, for turning on her as coldly as her father, for abandoning her the same way her mother had abandoned her? For making her feel lonelier and more unloved than she'd ever felt? She'd always asked for everything he'd given her. She'd finally grown up and learned that her mistake had been to believe in heroes. A woman had to have more than a curiosity about her sexuality and a thirst for love. She had to have her own courage, which she had lacked—till now.

Dear God. For too long she had allowed her life to be a cold, empty mansion, a husband who had never loved her, never slept with her, and a child who seemed to grow farther away from her every day. The aristocrats who were supposed to be her friends had never quite accepted her into their circle. They imagined they could tell the difference in what, to others, seemed flawless conduct but, to them, had been learned by art and imitation rather than from the cradle.

Lacy yanked together the curtains of the empty foyer. Sam was just upstairs in his bedroom, where he slept alone. She thought of her ten-year marriage and wondered, if she had never known Johnny Midnight, could she have been happy?

Johnny—why hadn't she looked past his incredible charm and seen how hard and cold he was at the core? From the moment he'd rescued her from her father, she'd craved him.

For a split second the ice around her heart cracked again as more of those unwanted but never to be forgotten memories swamped her. Johnny, embarrassed and blushing when she'd snuck down her fire escape and caught him in his bedroom at his parents' house devouring a seminude picture of a blonde who'd looked a lot like her. Johnny, laughingly placing a tinsel crown on her head and calling her his princess when she'd dressed up in her mother's old party clothes from a forgotten trunk in her attic. Johnny, promising her he'd love her forever.

Johnny stubbornly clinging to his own truths and unfeeling to her own terror and loss and pain.

Johnny, ruthlessly violating both her body and soul in that last, final act of vengeance.

Don't look back. Don't remember... Johnny. Not any more. He isn't worth it. He never was.

She shouldn't hate him the way she did because he had cruelly destroyed all that was tender and young and adventurous in her forever when he'd cast her aside. She shouldn't hold him responsible for the long, empty years. He was a mistake; *Sam* had been a mistake. Two terrible mistakes *she* had made. She had to forget the past and forge a new and more meaningful life herself, for herself—without a man.

But there was a vital, living reason, closer to her heart than the past, why she'd never be able to forget Johnny Midnight.

Lacy's heels echoed in the empty house before they sank into the plush rugs. She glided toward a low table and picked up a crystal ashtray the staff had missed. Sam had seemed on edge all night. He hadn't complimented her on tonight's party. Not that she'd cared. Nor had she cared when he'd complained that the freshly shot fowl he had demanded she order had failed to arrive.

Lacy Douglas didn't care about pleasing her difficult husband any more. She was leaving him.

The shadowy emptiness of her house seemed to seep into her. Lightning cracked, and for a split second the cold perfection of the grand living room that she had furnished so painstakingly in early European furniture was revealed—Jacobean commodes and armchairs with wine-colored tapestry seats, wide sofas and chairs upholstered in maroon and white. Priceless art hung on the walls. The twin Delft chandeliers sparkled eerily over her grand piano as she passed beneath them on her way to the kitchen with the ashtray.

On her way back she hesitated before the piano she always kept locked. Once she'd sung popular arias at Sam's parties—Puccini, *Madama Butterfly*. No more.

Now her treasured piano was covered with rows of precisely spaced silver-framed pictures that included several of

Lacy and Sam with the president and first lady. Others were signed pictures of European royalty. Behind the cluster of celebrity shots, there were only two of the Douglas family.

Her fingertips lingered on the one of her twin stepchildren. They were only six years younger than she was. The shot had been taken before her marriage to Sam. Colleen and Cole were in the pool, laughing, happier than she'd ever seen them. No one had guessed then how seriously disturbed Cole really was, how unloved and neglected he must have felt.

Her wedding picture was harder to look at. She lifted the piano bench and stuffed the photograph inside facedown. She'd been so sick that day, she'd barely made it down the aisle.

She set the burglar alarm, turned off the lights, climbed the stairs and locked herself into her vast darkened bedroom.

The servants didn't sleep in the main house. Neither did her son, Joe, and the mansion was so huge that Lacy was always a little afraid. She locked the connecting door to her husband's bedroom as well. Then she crossed the silvery darkness, going to her gilt mirror where she took off the heavy tiara and shook out her hair. The pins that had held it in place came loose and showered onto the white carpet. She leaned down and carefully collected them, one by one. Just as carefully she slid her wedding band off and dropped it in her jewelry box.

Tomorrow she was leaving. She'd left before, but Sam had always forced her back.

Never again. The old threats wouldn't work, even though she felt sorry for him. For a while he would probably be lost without her—until he found someone else to play the part.

She knew he was in some kind of trouble, although she didn't know what. He'd always been distrustful, and the higher he'd climbed the more secrets he'd kept from her.

Telephone calls came at odd hours. If she answered, the caller hung up. White envelopes addressed to Sam were hand delivered by special courier several times a month. One had come earlier tonight. Lacy wondered if he was being blackmailed. She knew the IRS was investigating his affairs.

Sam had always known how to get what he wanted, who he could buy.

She shivered. *He had known how to get her, how to keep her—against her will.*

Her temple pounded as she knelt beside her bed and drew out the small leather suitcase she'd packed and hidden.

Tomorrow would be her new beginning. And Joe's.

When she turned on the lamp by her bed, she gasped in shock at the torn white envelope and newspaper clippings someone had scattered wildly across her glazed chintz spread.

One headline stood out.

Cole Douglas escapes mental institution.

Beneath the headline she read that he had spent months chipping concrete away from an air vent with a plastic knife, that he'd carried the dirt out in his pockets every time he got a recreation break.

Some sharp instrument had gouged deep holes through the newsprint and into the spread. Her hand began to shake as she skimmed the rest of the clippings.

"Still considered very dangerous...very unstable...a threat to himself as well as to others. Believed to be on his way to Virginia where his father, Senator Sam Douglas resides with his much younger wife, Lacy Douglas."

Surely Sam must know.

Why hadn't he told her?

Lacy wondered if Cole's twin, Colleen, knew about this. She was now an aspiring actress in Los Angeles. Lacy would have to call and warn her.

The writer mentioned the fire, how Cole had his first breakdown the same night his mother had died.

Lacy pulled on a negligee. She had never really known Cole. But she'd been close to Colleen, who had suffered terribly after her mother's death and Cole's breakdown.

Lacy was about to throw on her peignoir and take the clippings into Sam when she heard a low, garbled sound. The red light of the intercom by her bed flashed. Static crackled. When Sam slept at home, as a polite formality, he always told her good-night over the intercom.

She leaned down and waited for her husband's voice. No need to see him face-to-face. She would ask him about the clippings now.

But the voice wasn't Sam's, and interference from the storm chopped the whisper into squawks of barely recognizable words and phrases.

"You should . . . have sent the money."

Some threatening quality in the low tone sent a trill of fear down her spine.

Then a violent gust of wind shook the windowpanes.

She heard Sam's voice, throaty, terrified. "I'm through doling out— You! Get out!"

Was Cole already here? Was he blackmailing Sam?

"There's no statute of limitations for murder. . . . Do you really want people to know what happened when the warehouse burned?"

Lacy's breath caught.

Sam couldn't have had anything to do with the fire. . . . Her whole absurd life had been built on that naive belief.

She was paralyzed, her mind racing back to her graduation night when she and Johnny had returned home, satiated with each other, stunned to see that ominous fiery light in the sky, only to watch disbelievingly as the paramedics tended Midnight's horribly injured father and then wheeled two bagged bodies out of the smoking ruins of the Douglas warehouse.

Johnny had said the Douglases framed his father. And she had refused to believe him.

The wind howled beneath the eaves. Livid white explosions made the sky pulse like strobe lights. She felt hot and cold as she backed away from the intercom.

Sam's choked, broken voice. "I don't want the truth to come out . . . Cole . . . can't pay any longer."

Lacy's hand closed over her mouth. Her husband's words ate through her like acid. She didn't want to hear. She didn't want to know. She saw Johnny's ravaged face when she'd refused to believe him about the Douglases.

Sam wheezed, as if he were having one of his asthmatic attacks. "I need . . . air . . ."

"I'll give you air—breathe through your guts."

A table was knocked over. A lamp crashed against the parquet floor, smashing the priceless antique-crystal base.

Bodies slammed against the wall with shuddering force. Then a gun exploded and a bullet ripped through the connecting door, splintering wood and whizzing so close to Lacy's cheek she felt the air stir.

Her mirror shattered.

She screamed.

Then she heard a feverish, crazed laugh. "Slim's next. . . ."

". . . bastard . . ."

"Then Joe—my baby brother. It'll be fun."

"You're a psycho."

"You should have figured that out a long time ago. Nighty night, *Daddy.*"

The killer's gun and the night sky exploded at the same time. Against the blaze of white, the trees near the house stood out starkly against the bitter landscape.

All the lights in the house went out.

Sam made a horrible gurgling sound. Something fell heavily against the connecting door and slid to the floor.

There was an awful waiting silence.

Lightning flared. Petrified, Lacy saw the dreadful glimmer of something wet and dark seeping beneath the door, staining her white carpet.

Sam's blood. She had to help him. Sinking to her knees, she was crawling toward the door when the knob turned.

Dear God! He was going to kill her, too.

The knob twisted violently and jammed.

A fist banged against the wood. "Damn...you..." A fiendish whisper. "Slim, open the door. I know you're there."

Lacy's nails clawed the carpet. "Sam..."

No answer.

"Sam!"

There was only the fury of the wind, and when even that stopped someone's heart thundered deafeningly.

Her own.

The world seemed to stop spinning. *Sam was dead.*

Time froze.

"No..."

"I'll get you, and Joe, too. Sooner or later."

Joe! Lacy had to save her son. A feeling of suffocating panic closed around her as she grabbed her small suitcase, her purse and keys, and raced toward the window. She opened it and climbed onto the veranda, expecting a monstrous hand to coil out of the darkness and grab her.

Instead the blue-black snub-nosed barrel of a .38 revolver smashed through Sam's window. Then a black leg thrust over the windowsill. Lacy screamed and ran.

Forty seconds after the glass broke, the alarm went off. A dozen lights blinked on in the cottage. More lights came on along the high wall that surrounded the estate. The guard dogs leapt out of their dog houses and roamed the grounds in howling packs. Even though she was afraid of the Dobermans, Sam had taught her that they knew her and wouldn't hurt her.

Icy rain soaked through her thin nightgown as she raced toward the cottage Joe shared with his Austrian governess and the other servants. For once she was thankful that Sam had never allowed him to live in the main house.

She heard something behind her in the grass, something pounding the damp earth heavily, leaping after her.

She had reached the cottage.

As she climbed the stairs, the thudding grew louder.

She banged desperately on the cottage door.

From behind her there was a roaring in her ears.

I'll get you, and Joe, too. Sooner or later.

Cowering against the door, she turned to face her killer.

A big black demon with barred dagger-sharp teeth and fiery eyes leapt through the curtain of black rain into the golden light of the porch—straight at her throat.

She shut her eyes and screamed. *"Cole!"*

Nothing happened.

Something slobbery and stinky warm slopped her face like a dirty mop. She opened her eyes and saw that it was only one of the big black Dobermans—Nero, the one whose ear had been chewed off when he was just a pup. He shook his glossy coat, drenching her. Then, as if he thought himself presentable, he lowered his head, wagging his tail sheepishly. His brown eyes were shy as he warily sniffed her trembling white hand.

She sank to her knees, throwing her arms around his thick, smelly neck. The monster's big tongue washed her a second time. Then the door opened, and she was inside along with her leaping new friend, gathering Joe into her arms even when he acted tough and stubbornly fought to shrug her off.

And running.

Running for both their lives.

And the big, leaping one-eared monster raced after them.

Three

Lacy Douglas was in San Francisco. She was in terrible trouble. J.K. said she needed him.

She'd betrayed him.

Johnny Midnight's red sports car roared past the Presidio at a speed that made his blood rush. He was driving way too fast. But what the hell? His Italian sports car had been built for speed. More importantly, his feelings were explosive, and he'd felt trapped in the city.

No, what really trapped him was that stupid character glitch that made him want to play hero even when it came to a rich conniver such as Lacy, who'd broken his heart ten years ago.

J. K. Cameron, his best friend and boss, knew his flaw. He had deliberately baited him when he'd told him that Sam had been murdered and Lacy was being hunted by someone. Her crazy stepson, Cole, who'd escaped from that fancy private mental institution where he'd been warehoused for years, was wanted for questioning. These facts didn't quite wash.

Just for a second, Johnny wondered what Lacy was like now. Was she as beautiful and golden as her photographs in the social columns and magazines? Was she happy?

Why the hell did he give a damn? But old emotions that were supposed to be dead built like an explosive gas inside him, and he felt as if hands were pressing against his chest, cutting off the blood to his pounding heart. Suddenly he couldn't breathe.

No... He couldn't remember her. So, he remembered Cole instead. Which meant remembering Colleen, whom Midnight didn't want to remember either. They'd had vivid red hair and equally vivid blue eyes. They'd been wild, difficult kids, given everything in the world except what they really needed—their glamorous parents' attention. In the two years Midnight had worked weekends at the Douglases' mansion, he'd never seen the Douglases go out as a family—except that terrible night when Camella had died.

Midnight had become their weekend baby-sitter one Saturday morning when his sleep had been shattered by their real baby-sitter's piercing screams. The eleven-year-old monsters had shoved her out a third-story window and were gleefully dangling her by her ankles, too weak to pull her back inside. He'd rushed into the main house and saved her. Then he'd lowered the little hellions out the same window and held them both there, pulling them to safety only after the baby-sitter had begged him to. After that it hadn't been too hard for him to control them.

Funny, how he'd always figured Colleen to be the kid with twisted passions and ideas, the leader. Cole had definitely been the follower.

Well, you could never tell about people—they were too unpredictable.

He'd damn sure been wrong about Lacy.

Still, it was hard to imagine Cole blowing Sam away on his own.

But then his old man hadn't seemed much like your typical murderer, either. The Douglases were good at hiding things.

Like father, like son.

And Lacy had betrayed him first by moving in with them and then by marrying into that family.

Midnight's thoughts returned to J. K. Cameron. Who the hell did J.K. think he was, meddling in Midnight's life by helping Lacy?

The car cut through the wind on a soaring purr. The Golden Gate whipped past.

Damn J.K. No one was more tenacious than J.K. about clinging to a grudge of his own. Why couldn't he remember that Slim had carved out a big piece of Midnight's soul with her betrayal ten years ago? She'd as good as sold him to the devil. She'd left him behind and married Sam because he could offer her the world and Midnight could only give her his heart. She'd had no fear of murder then. She'd sworn she believed Sam was innocent.

Because of her style, she'd been the perfect politician's wife, a great favorite in Washington. Midnight had read articles about her perfect sense of style, her perfect houses, her perfect friends. Somewhere he'd read she'd had a son. He pitied the poor kid. No doubt she and Sam had ignored him the same way Sam had ignored his first two. There had been lavish spreads in newspapers and magazines about her home. Nothing much was ever written about the kid.

She'd wanted to be a princess.

Midnight had just wanted her to need him.

She'd needed him and used him till she'd discovered the Douglases could help her more. Then she'd tossed him aside so easily he'd known he'd never meant anything to her. He'd just been a lowly rung on the ladder of her monumental ambition.

She'd called him once, a month after she'd married. By then Midnight had recovered enough to remind her she was married and to go to hell before he'd hung up. She'd had her kid, and he'd never heard from her again.

Not that he'd ever wanted to. They had nothing in common. He wasn't for sale the way she was.

Midnight veered off the freeway. Instead of taking the road to Sausalito and his houseboat, he swerved onto the coast road to Stinson Beach.

There was a lot of traffic in Tam Junction, but it thinned out when he turned left and headed into the hills. The highway climbed through pungent eucalyptus trees and aromatic pines, snaking upward for several miles. The vegetation thinned as the car snarled up the brown barren hills. After a while there were panoramic views of the startlingly blue Pacific, of a distant glistening San Francisco, but Midnight didn't notice.

He drove faster, more anxious than ever to get to Stinson and stare out at the horizon and watch the endless crash of waves as they rolled in from the Pacific. He wanted to forget the one woman he couldn't forget.

There wasn't much traffic in his lane although a steady stream of cars was in the oncoming lane, heading back to the city. Without thinking Midnight accelerated on a curve. On his right was brown hill; on his left, sheer cliffs plummeted to a rocky shore. Behind him a blue Toyota tailgated too closely.

J.K. had said Slim was running for her life. Sam was dead, her perfect life at the top of the world was over.

If ever a grasping bitch deserved to be in trouble—Midnight's fist flinched on the wheel as he remembered J.K.'s last question.

"But does she deserve to die?"

How the hell would it be his fault if something happened to her?

He ground the accelerator to the floorboard.

Too late he saw the yellow car and then the van that was trying to pass it. The van—monstrous and huge, loomed in front of him in his lane, barreling toward him head-on. There was a turnout on the opposite side of the road. Why hadn't the bastard in the yellow car used it?

Cliffs hemmed him in on the right. All Midnight could do was swerve directly across the path of the oncoming yellow car.

He spun his wheel to the left and gunned it.

A tiny horn made a faraway sound.

His sports car missed the yellow sedan by a millimeter, striking the guardrail instead, bouncing off it, skidding and hitting it again.

Fancy Kevlar wrap peeled off his fender. He jammed his foot down hard on the brake. For a second he thought everything was going to be okay. Then the blue Toyota rammed him violently from the back. The impact snapped the flimsy guardrail, and he was hurtling through it, over the cliff.

Blue sky and blue water came together and blurred. The highest tips of the Golden Gate Bridge stuck through the swirl of fog like orange spikes. He saw the cliff's edge. And then nothingness.

He was going to die.

His life didn't pass in front of him. Instead he was twenty, standing beneath the eaves of the Douglas guest house behind their pool, and Slim was with him, her white dress damp and clingy. He'd kissed a raindrop off the tip of her nose, and that had led to the rest. He'd taken her innocence, but he'd given her his unconditional love and promised her he'd love her forever. She'd promised him, too. But that had been before the fire. Before Sam. Before she'd seen a way to profit from them both. Before her true character had been revealed.

Then he saw her that last afternoon when he'd taken her violently and thrown her out forever.

She'd been unforgettably lovely to him, despite his knowledge that she had secretly tricked him into accepting money from Sam to ease her own guilty conscience because she was doing so well herself.

She had lain in Midnight's arms, her tiny white hands seductively interwoven through his. Her white-gold hair had been tangled from his lovemaking. She had not acted the least bit guilty for having sold herself to the man whom Midnight had told her he suspected of murdering his own wife and both their fathers. He'd known then that her father had been right all along—she was like her mother, willing to sell herself to the highest bidder no matter who he was.

So he'd cut her in the cruelest way he could think of and stalked out of her life forever. And he'd stuck to his black opinion for ten years, never listening to any argument in her defense nor to his own niggling subconscious doubts. Never letting himself dwell on the recurring vision he'd had of a skinny, lost-looking little girl who'd needed love more than anybody he'd ever known.

Now in that last conscious second before oblivion he wondered if he'd been wrong. No matter how hard he'd tried, he'd never stopped loving her, even when he hated her. She'd aroused the darkest emotions in his soul, but she'd aroused the brightest ones, too.

The years without her had been dead and empty. She was the only thing in his life worth living for, the only thing worth dying for.

And he'd thrown it all away.

More than anything in the world he wanted a second chance.

His car hit rock and bounced. Metal groaned, but the steel subframes that welded the passenger compartment held.

The car hit rock again, and his bucket seat tore loose. He was thrown so violently against the steering wheel that his shoulder harness broke, and his head crashed into the windshield, shattering the glass.

He was already unconscious as shards of broken glass embedded themselves in his dark brow. The car rolled crumpling in upon itself like an accordion, and it catapulted crazily toward the cliff's razor edge, which fell hundreds of feet to an angry swirl of white-foamed surf.

Above him a black-cloaked figure smiled and got back into a blue Toyota and drove away.

Funny, how Midnight, the tough guy who'd grown up hard on cruel inner-city streets, Midnight who'd had to fight with his fists and his wits for his very survival in those foul, garbage-strewn back alleys, had never let on that deep down he was weak and needy and afraid, a coward—unlike his brother, Nathan, who'd been a true hero. Nathan, their father's favorite, who had died young and left his unworthy brother behind to face a tough world alone.

No, Midnight had never let on that the reason he'd always been so damned good at fighting was because he was so damned scared of dying. He'd always had to be the fighter, the rescuer, the strong one, the hero, so nobody would guess he was really a coward. So no one would guess that deep down he wasn't at all like his older brother.

Midnight had thought death meant blackness forever, helplessness, nothingness, his body imprisoned in a coffin the way Nathan's had been, and then buried and forgotten. Midnight had always been afraid of the darkness, of being shut in. Growing up, he'd had nightmares about Nathan.

But death wasn't like that. It was kind of nice in a weird way.

Midnight wasn't in a coffin. He was flying—high in a sunlit silence. Instead of darkness there was brilliant light and glorious freedom and an incredible weightlessness of being.

His whole senseless life had been about pretending he was
a hero when he wasn't, and now at last all those games were
over and he felt at peace. The world beneath him seemed
quiet and he glided above the tangled wreckage of a toy car
that teetered precariously on the cliff's edge. A soundless
wind ruffled the gauzy azure sea and stirred the brown
grasses. At first he didn't recognize his car. Nor did he realize the lifeless body crushed inside it was his own.

Then he flew closer and saw the blood in the black hair,
the twisted broken shape of the man crushed inside the car,
and he remembered how crazy fast he'd been driving. But
even when he got smart and figured out that must be his
body, he felt no pain because he was free, and all the fighting was over at last. An ever-widening blossom of fire was
sucking him away from the car into a tunnel of light at an
incredibly exhilarating speed.

More than anything he wanted to get to the end of the
tunnel, but a man with white hair who wore a red bathrobe
blocked his way. The man glowed strangely like a giant
Japanese lantern lighted from the inside by a candle. The
only thing about him that didn't glow were the five black
holes etched into his gut. He didn't speak, but he didn't have
to. Midnight recognized his old boss, his old enemy and ri-
val instantly—Sam Douglas—and he could read his
thoughts. Sam silently commanded him to go back.

Let me by.

Sam shook his head. *You've got to save Lacy.*

Then Midnight saw his father and his mother and his
brother, Nathan. They were okay after all. They wanted him
to go back, too. After that he didn't fight so hard against the
invisible force pulling him back through the tunnel.

Midnight felt the pain then, savage bolts of it everywhere
like burning knife blades popping into his body from all di-
rections, but most of all the blades were gouging into his
head, into his forehead. He was sucked through that tunnel, back into the poor, battered, almost lifeless creature in
the car. Back into a semiconscious state that was pain and

loss and terror. He felt the weight of a thousand pounds of metal crushing down on his chest. He wanted to get up and fly again, but he was trapped.

He wanted space. Instead he knew panic. He was shut in. Trapped.

After a while he heard voices. Welders with torches were working to cut him free. Every time they shifted the metal wreckage, they caused him more agony than before.

He didn't want to be trapped in a broken body. He prayed for death.

He passed out instead.

Hours later Midnight awoke to gloved hands probing his head and chest. Needles stabbed him everywhere. His clothes had been cut from his body and he lay beneath an electric coverlet that kept him warm. Bright lights blazed from the ceiling. People in white were talking in fast, urgent whispers. He was aware of one doctor in particular—because her hands slipped and she dropped her scalpel.

The pain seemed to come from within his body, and it was sharper than any of the surgeons' needles or knives. It seemed to him that every nerve in his head was shot through with needles and glass.

He tried to talk, to tell them that he wanted to die.

Instead their masked faces were lost in darkness.

When the lights came back on, the doctors were screaming to each other, frantic now. "We're losing him...."

He wasn't lost. He was out of his body, soaring free again, free of the pain and the darkness, hovering above them, watching them disinterestedly while they struggled feverishly.

He felt sorry for that female neurosurgeon, though. She was tall and slim, and she had intense, terrified brown eyes. Midnight noted her hand shook with a fine tremor as everyone held their breath and watched as she ever so gently did her work.

Then Midnight went through a wall and found himself in a hospital waiting room. Lacy was there, alone, in tears. For ten years he'd believed her heart was made of ice, that she didn't care whether he lived or died, that she'd married Sam for his money.

In a microsecond he knew he'd been wrong.

She was white and trembling and praying silently for him to live, her whole heart and soul in her prayers. He came down beside her and tried to speak, to comfort her, to tell her death wasn't all that bad. For an instant she started and looked wildly around as if she somehow sensed his presence. But she couldn't see him or hear him, and common sense persuaded her she was crazy to think he was there. Her grief became more desperate than before.

More than anything Midnight had ever wanted, he wanted to talk to her, to touch her—just one last time. To tell her that he was sorry for hurting her, for leaving her.

For being wrong.

But, first, he had to live.

In a distant part of the same city, in an elegant hotel room, a solitary cloaked figure dressed in black sat hunched in silent anguish over an antique tea table, slim hands pressed together begging the Devil to curse Johnny Midnight and make him die an excruciating death while Lacy watched.

Or better yet—let his brilliant mind be reduced to vegetative pulp so Lacy would pity him and he would despise himself.

Let them learn what it was like to feel powerless, unloved, and unlovable. They who had never suffered, deserved to suffer.

A photograph album and a rusty lighter lay together in a pool of dying sunlight. *Trophies. Memories.*

Slim fingers lifted the album and flipped pages. There was no need to dwell on the precisely-ordered photographs because every hated one was branded into the twisted soul of the person in the room.

First came the publicity photographs of the *perfect* Douglas family in their *perfect* home. The four of them— the radiant, dark-haired Camella, the famous senator, and their two children—attractively posed like a normal loving family around their pool or dinner table, activities they'd never shared in real life.

After the publicity shots came grainy black-and-white pictures. Camella's pet spaniel, Muffy, was swimming in the pool, swimming frantically because the water level had been lowered so he couldn't get out. The next picture was his sodden, furry shape at the bottom of the pool. Another was of Camella and her lover. The loveliest was of Midnight.

There were no pictures of the long lonely hours spent shut in dark closets, feeling unloved, wishing the darkness was death.

The slim gloved hand jerked angrily to the famous newspaper clipping of Sam holding Lacy in front of the fire, ripped the hated thing out and flicked the lighter, setting Lacy's paper face on fire.

The acrid smell of smoke brought back the glory of *that night*.

Not that the glory had lasted. Johnny Midnight hadn't believed his father was to blame and he'd caused others to wonder as well. Worst of all beautiful, charismatic Lacy had come into the family. She had made smashing copy in all the newspapers—her glories eclipsing that of the fire. Everybody had loved her.

Not everybody.

Now Lacy was with Johnny again.

Which meant that they both had to die.

The last pages in the album were blank. More clippings were needed.

A story this good deserved a gloriously spectacular ending.

And the cloaked figure felt like God.

Four

———

When Midnight woke up a week after the accident, his head was wrapped in thick white bandages. He had vague memories of a woman's voice, a beautiful voice, reading to him, singing to him; a voice that stirred painful, haunting memories and yet made him want to live.

His nose was broken. His left leg was in a cast. He lay in a semilucid state, not knowing who he was or where he was. He didn't remember the accident. He'd forgotten how to swallow and he couldn't understand much of the English language. What he did understand only added to his agony and terror.

One word in particular penetrated the haze of drugs and pain to terrify him.

Vegetable. It was the first he understood.

Never before had he known that such a simple, innocent word could be the most terrible word in the English language. It seemed to pound upon his aching brain, shouting louder and more distinctly than all the other unintelligible rushes of sounds.

Where was he? What was wrong with him? Would he ever be himself—whatever *that* had been—again?

Mercifully the pain and the drugs kept the terror of that word and his future at bay most of the time while he recovered. His pain smothered him, enveloped him and cut him off from the world. At the same time, it was the only thing that made him know he was still alive. And in spite of his new terrors, he wanted to live, to get well, with a fierce will he couldn't comprehend because at the same time he despised himself for being so pitiful and helpless—for being a coward.

He had terrible nightmares. Sometimes he grew smaller and smaller until he was a sniveling, cowardly little kid again. The monster he was so scared of—Nathan called it a raptaroo—had flown into the house. Midnight was hiding in that dark closet—so terrified he wouldn't come out, but he could hear Nathan fighting the thing, its hideous prehistoric wings flapping as his brother battled for both their lives.

Then Midnight was older, and the bullies were chasing him down dark alleys, taunting him because Nathan was dead now, calling him a coward. They got him down and sliced him open from the shoulder to his belly and left him for dead in the gutter.

His nightmares had a familiar quality. He didn't know he'd had them ever since Nathan had been run over on his bike and his father had stared morosely into his coffin and said, "My good son is dead. All I've got left is the coward."

The first month Midnight was barely conscious. The second month passed in a sort of bleary confusion of dark days and darker nights. A lot of the time Midnight was too desperately ill to tell one from the other.

He had one overriding, despicable emotion—fear. Even when Dr. Lescuer came and reassured him, he felt it.

Fear that he was going to be weak and helpless and alone forever.

Teams of consulting doctors spoke in long words of anterograde and retrograde amnesia, but the doctors were difficult to understand. Midnight was too tired to answer their questions.

Olga Martinez, the night nurse was easier to understand. She was the first person to use that word that could penetrate his hellish darkness and throbbing pain even during that first month.

Vegetable.

She whispered it into his ear, repeating, so that it crept into those dark gaps in his mind to fester while he lay semiconscious, helplessly tied to life-supporting machines like some freak in a mad scientist's laboratory. Since he knew his brain wasn't working properly, he was terrified she was right.

Olga, the fat night nurse whose huge hands felt like ice, was guilty of other cruelties. She liked massaging him roughly with those cold hands until he writhed in pain. She'd tied him down after he'd pulled out his IV, telling everyone he was too dangerous to have visitors. So, the beautiful woman with the haunting voice hadn't come again.

Olga savored her power over him because she was a cold-blooded tyrant, and he was helpless. He knew all about bullies from growing up in a rough neighborhood. When he'd been small, they'd terrorized him. There was no Nathan to save him now. But Midnight would get even with her, as he'd gotten even with them. All he had to do was wait.

As he slowly improved, his life-support systems were removed. He relearned how to swallow, how to talk, how to walk on a walker in spite of his cast.

Then one night Olga cut his pain medication so that his muscles writhed for hours in pulsing spasms. When she came in the middle of the night and leaned close, he tried to twist away, only to be held fast by the straps that tied him down. Softly she snarled the hateful word against his ear.

Vegetable.

Rage made his heart pound. Then his muscular body jerked against the leather straps, and she laughed. Which made him so angry he spit in her face.

She picked up his pillow and laid it over his face, pressing downward very hard.

He thrashed wildly, fighting to stay conscious. The world was blackening when one of the straps on his wrists broke. His hand lashed out, grabbing her throat.

She started screaming. "Orderly! Orderly! Disruptive patient! B23!"

His fingers tightened.

"Lunatic!" she hissed.

Doors banged. There were running footsteps down that long hall. He winced as her rescuing troops fell heavily upon him. Razorlike pain exploded in his brain and in his chest when they pushed against his three fractured ribs.

Their bodies weighed so much he couldn't breathe. Their faces blurred. He could barely fight them as they added more straps and buckled them so tightly they cut off the circulation to his wrists and ankles. Then *she* moved gleefully toward him with a loaded syringe.

"This should zonk him."

When he clawed the arms that pinioned him, she laughed softly.

His hospital room door opened again.

A slim, defiant figure was framed in the doorway. The light came from behind her and made her white-gold hair gleam like an angel's aureole. Midnight felt a new ripple of electrifying tension race through the room.

"Excuse me." The feminine voice was velvety soft, but it snapped like a whip, cutting into him with a crueler force than his fear or the biting straps and buckles that bound him.

His captors froze.

So did he.

It was the most beautiful voice, he'd ever heard. The voice he'd remembered when he'd first regained consciousness. But, God, how the sound of it hurt—worse than anything had ever hurt him.

Something warm and vital and nostalgic and yet, at the same time, something powerfully, negatively charged, something larger than memory—an emotion that held hunger, need, and profound loss as well as betrayal—came sharply alive and coursed through him.

Who was she?

He wanted to run. He wanted to die. Most of all he didn't want this glamorous being to see what a pitiful wretch he'd become, but since he couldn't escape, Midnight forced himself to stare at her.

Every eye in the room followed suit.

She was tall and golden, exquisitely groomed in white silk and gold accessories. She didn't look evil. No, she looked like a fairy princess, his very own fairy princess, his very own avenging angel.

She was his enemy, his killer, his destroyer. He didn't want her fighting on his side.

She had violet eyes and ash blond hair, and although she was more elegant than beautiful, she would stand out, even in a room filled with more beautiful women. Her delicate oval face was beautifully shaped, and her head exquisitely placed on her long slim neck. Her pale skin had some radiant quality that seemed to draw all the light in the room and then reflect it back. But it was her enormous, luminous eyes that captivated a man, that hinted at hidden vulnerabilities and secret passions and sorrows.

Who was she? Why did her beauty fill him with fierce hatred and bitter longing? Why was it so intensely shaming for him to have her see him like this?

Beside his bed Dr. Lescuer had erected a bulletin board. Every morning she pinned pictures and messages that were supposed to mean something to him. There was even one of his mangled car. He never responded to Dr. Lescuer when she came to see him, but after she left he studied the bulletin board and thought about the things she had said.

Your name is Johnny Riggs Midnight. You are at Belle Vista Hospital. Today is October 14. You had a car accident. You were brought in on August 19. You are thirty-five years old. You are a lawyer. You work for J. K. Cameron.

Every morning Dr. Lescuer had added new photographs and new lists of confusing facts about himself which he tried to read when no one was watching. It was terribly hard to focus, to concentrate. On the first day he could read, he'd stumbled over the words after she'd left him—Stanford Law. Phi Beta Kappa.

He'd been an expert at complex mergers and acquisitions. He could remember Stanford, but when it came to his work with mergers, his memories grew fuzzier. It was as if his easily distracted brain moved in slow motion. When he'd been at Stanford he'd wanted to do *pro bono* law, to work for the poor. Somewhere along the way, he'd sold out along with J.K., and together they'd spent their time getting very, very rich by buying companies that were in trouble and breaking them up.

Midnight knew he'd lost two months in the hospital. But they were nothing compared to the missing years and the gaps in the memories he did have, and his terror that he might never be able to fill in those blank places.

Light shimmered in the blond woman's hair, in her violet eyes. She triggered his worst fears about the blanks in his mind. He knew that once she'd been his goddess, and he'd

worshiped at her shrine. But somehow she'd proved herself
unworthy, and all his illusions had been shattered.

Once his heart had overflowed with love for her, but she
had used his love to destroy him.

*Maybe that was why Dr. Lescuer hadn't put a photo-
graph of her on his bulletin board.*

When the woman took a single step into the room, he
shrank against his pillow, shaking, somehow knowing that
she was more dangerous to him than ten thousand Olgas.

"Get her out of here," he growled violently in pitiful
broken syllables. "I—I don't want her here!"

She whitened. But she stayed, biting the inside of her lip
and summoning the courage to speak. "What exactly is going on here?"

*That voice again—frightened yet determined—as if
fighting were a new thing for her.*

He had loved her. And lost her. She'd been his princess.
She had betrayed him.

How the hell did he know that?

The night nurse waved her away with her syringe. "Get
her out of here."

An orderly rushed toward the young woman, grabbing
her roughly by a slender arm, shoving her against the wall
so hard she cried out.

"Damn you!" Midnight hissed, his words an incompre-
hensible snarl of more tangled syllables as he hurled himself against the straps in a vain attempt to free himself so he
could help her. What the hell made him want to rid himself
of her and yet at the same time protect her?

"Not so fast," came a deeper authoritative male tone behind the woman.

"Get security," the night nurse yelled wildly, frantic now
as J. K. Cameron stepped into the room.

*How come J.K. had turned traitor and come with the
blonde?*

"And while you're at it, get Dr. Lescuer on the phone," J.K. coolly commanded. "I want to know what's going on here."

"The patient is out of control," the night nurse spat in her most venomous tone.

The slim blonde shook herself free of the orderly and glided toward his bed with stately, furious grace.

"Excuse me," she whispered in that soft, defiant way of hers, pushing her way through the throng hovering around him.

Everyone stepped back except the sadistic night nurse who guarded Midnight as jealously as a dragon would her prey. "Lady, if you're smart, you'll go. He's vicious and dangerous." Olga's heavy voice was laden with censure.

"He's tied down. There are six of you. But even if I were alone with him, he wouldn't hurt me."

Her words made him feel like he was less than nothing.

The nurse's syringe flashed menacingly. "Not if I sedate him for you."

"Don't you dare touch him! I want to talk to him."

"Ha!" Olga snorted. "That won't be easy. He's not a man any more. He don't talk. He's a vegetable."

Despair closed over Midnight. The bitter fighting light went out of his eyes. His lids fell heavily, and he lay very still. He felt humiliated to the core, defeated. He wished he could shrivel up inside himself. The last thing he wanted was for this beautiful woman to see him weak and helpless, tied down like an animal, no longer a man. The last thing he wanted was to owe her anything.

"Don't say that!" the woman said to Olga. "If anyone's vicious or dangerous, it's you—" She broke off, her voice shaking. "Johnny, you're not a vegetable," she finished gently.

"Go to hell," he spat, not wanting her pity.

When she stubbornly took his limp hand and stroked it until the numbness was gone, he looked away and wouldn't respond. "Your brain scans don't even show damage. You're going to be okay. It's just going to take a little time."

Midnight scowled darkly, pretending not to understand her.

Just as she pretended his cold reaction didn't bother her and calmly took charge of him and everyone, ordering them all out of the room.

When J.K. led them out and Midnight, tied down, found himself alone with her, the tiny room seemed more like a prison than ever. When she leaned toward him, he was helpless to escape her. Very slowly she threaded her fingers through his.

And that brought the rush of poignant, dangerous memories. Of sunshine and flowers. Of nighttime. Of rain on her face. Of raindrops sliding down her nose, and of his lips kissing one drop away. Of wet, warm skin against skin; his sandpaper rough, hers slick and satiny smooth. Of ecstasy. Of tortured memories and tortured longings. Of profound love and profound loss. He'd lain on top of her, the heat of their bodies flowing together as if they were one. Afterward they'd lain together, their hands threaded together just as they were now, clinging.

The shock of their hands touching sizzled through them both.

"Johnny," she whispered. She was so close to him her gentle breath grazed his skin and brought a spiraling rush of tingling sensation. He drew back, hating her, despising himself—and tormented all the more because he couldn't remember enough to know why.

"It's me—Lacy. I'm going to leave you for a little while and talk to your doctor. Then I'll be back."

His hand, which had lain limply inside hers, gripped hers more fiercely. *"Lacy. Slim."*

A second shock of awareness, stronger than the first, rippled through them both.

She took a deep steadying breath. "Dear God . . ."

He opened his eyes all the way, and let them burn across her face. "D-don't...come back—Lacy. I don't want you."

A sob caught in her throat and she tried to pull away.

But his grip held hers like a vise. "Rain...drop..." He said. "Why do I remember raindrops? On your face? On your nose?"

And such exquisite tenderness?

A tear spilled out of her eyes and rolled down her face. She tried to smear it away, but it fell onto his cheek.

"Oh, Johnny..." Her voice was choked. She looked wildly away. "You've got to understand. This is hard, not just for you, but hard for me, too. I don't want to be here any more than you want me to be here. We hurt each other once, terribly, and it's been over between us for years and years. Look, I know I shouldn't have come. But I had to. I guess I decided there's no reason for us to be afraid of one another because we aren't in love any more. We can't ever hurt each other like that again." Another one of her tears splashed his dark face.

Then why was she crying?

Her words bounced off the wall like hollow sounds. They filled him with frustration and fury because he didn't remember a damn thing about her, really. Because they didn't communicate any of the real emotions that were pulling them to each other like a dangerous riptide underneath a glassy surface. Somehow he knew that once they had been almost perfectly matched in every way—physically, emotionally and spiritually—until something had torn them apart.

"Johnny, I want us to make our peace. I want to help you now...but only as a friend...."

"Bull—"

"I was leaving town in one of J.K.'s limousines. I was on my way to the airport with Joe—"

"Who the hell is Joe?"

Lacy looked away again, her wet eyes huge and very frightened. "Never mind about Joe," she whispered. "He doesn't matter."

But a frantic tremor went through her.

She was lying—again.

"Anyway, when I heard you'd been in an accident, that you might die, I came to say... goodbye."

"Well, get it over with, damn it. Say it and leave!"

"It's not that easy... knowing you're lying here—helpless. Knowing that you're tied down and that that nurse might come back... and do anything to you."

"Know this then—I prefer her to you!" Midnight closed his eyes to shut out the sudden pain in her sweet, sad face, pain that he had inflicted. But most of all to shut out the sheer voluptuous beauty of her long, graceful neck and full-bosomed figure and to hide his own response to her. "Go on. Pretend I'm dead. That's why you came—to gloat over me like a vulture. You're just staying now because you've decided it's more fun to devour me alive."

Her delicate complexion paled. Her lashes fluttered. "You're wrong. I stayed with you day and night the first week, reading to you, talking to you. But when you came out of your coma, they wouldn't let me see you any more. They said you were too dangerous."

Lacy was so close to him, her soft silver hair wafted against his cheek. He breathed in her perfume.

He forced a bitter, derisive smile. "Just go."

Her violet eyes were luminous with tears. "Johnny—I know you probably think I've had the perfect life—"

Her throbbing voice sent unwanted fire through his veins.

"Johnny, there's no such thing as perfect."

Midnight's mouth hardened. "What makes you think I give a damn about your life? Just get out of mine."

Grimly she tried to nod, but her strength deserted her. When she started to back away from him, her beautiful, graceful figure seemed caught by some sharp, almost paralyzing tension.

"I—I'm not . . . a vegetable," he whispered.

He winced at the profound pity in her eyes, at her quick, tremulous smile to hide it, to reassure him. Then he struggled to pull his hand loose.

"You're right, Johnny," she said softly. "You're going to get well. Everything's going to be just fine. And the last thing you need is me around to complicate things. I don't guess we ever were very good for each other."

When his intent black gaze fastened on her face, he saw the sudden rigidity in her eyes, the fear that he would say more and cause her more pain. Something deeper than distrust, something more profound than hatred made his next words gentler.

"Yeah, we were all wrong for each other, Slim. But it felt good, didn't it—for a while? So damned good it fooled us both. It's hard to let go of things that feel that good." He held on to her for a long moment before relaxing his hand.

She was more shaken by this change in him than by any of his cruelties. A mask slid over her vulnerable features. Quickly she unthreaded her fingers from his.

Then she was gone, running away on swift, light feet. And his black loneliness and the inner terror-filled darkness in his slow-moving mind were ten times more hellish without her.

Five

Lacy leaned across Dr. Lescuer's large rectangular desk the next evening. "I'm sorry. I don't understand why Johnny has to be tied down like that."

"I told you. Because—"

But before Innocence could explain again, her telephone rang jarringly and she grabbed it, placing her hand over the mouthpiece.

"Excuse me. I really do have to catch this." Innocence frowned as she listened a minute and then lowered her voice and began to dictate swift, urgent orders, apparently to a nurse in O.R.

It was almost eleven in the evening, and Lacy knew that Dr. Lescuer had been at the hospital most of the night in acute care with a critical patient. Although Innocence was probably exhausted, her posture was correct and her demeanor calm, her quick voice carefully controlled. She was well-groomed and her light makeup perfectly applied. Her red hair was swept up from her face and secured in a tight gleaming knot on top of her head. Her stethoscope dangled from the crisp white collar of her medical jacket.

Most people probably saw what Innocence wanted them to see—a tireless, selfless doctor who was always in control. Lacy saw that behind Innocence's glasses dark smudges of weariness shadowed her big brown eyes. She saw a woman who rarely smiled, a woman who seemed merely to be going through the motions of life, a woman from whom some mysterious tragedy had exacted a terrible toll. Lacy understood too well.

Innocence set down the phone. Her shoulders slumped before she caught herself and straightened. When she looked up slowly, it took her a second to focus on Lacy. "I'm sorry. Another seriously injured patient has been brought in and is being prepped for surgery. You were saying—"

"Why does Johnny have to be tied down like an animal?"

Innocence removed her glasses and set them on top of her clipboard and rubbed her temples. The circles beneath her brown eyes were almost darker than her eyes. She leaned forward too, her tired voice not quite so professional. "So he won't hurt himself, Mrs. Douglas."

"I don't like that big nurse, Olga."

"Ms. Martinez comes on a little strong at times, but she has worked on this kind of ward for twenty years. Sometimes patients with head injuries need a firm hand."

"She's mean."

"Can you be more specific, Mrs. Douglas?"

"No, I—I can't. I just know mean. I grew up with mean."

"So did I. So did Olga." There was a crack in the cool professional tone, more concern in the weary gaze. Dr. Lescuer tried to smile as she lifted Midnight's thick chart from the stack and thumbed through it. "I remember the way you sat by him day and night when he was in a coma. You seem to care about him very much."

Lacy pressed her hands together tightly and stared down at her lap. "No, not really."

"Mr. Midnight is very important to me, too, Mrs. Douglas. I wish you could stay and be with him—just a few more days. He seems to respond to you."

"You mean that I make him furious."

"I admit—you do arouse his fighting instincts, but that is not an unusual response in cases like this. When I made rounds this morning he talked of nothing but you and your visit last night."

"You mean he ranted. I'm sure he was very hostile."

"But that's what was so wonderful! It was the first time he's ever spoken to me. You should have seen him. His skills with language are far better than I realized. He was passionate, even eloquent. . . ."

"I'll bet."

"He demanded to know why your picture wasn't on the bulletin board. I said because there hadn't been any of you in his boxes of pictures. Nor in his albums. He showed an interest in my questions, in everything. For the first time I feel certain he will make a full recovery. Now he wants to know who he is, who you are, why he feels the way he does. Only you can tell him, Mrs. Douglas."

Something cold curled deep inside Lacy as she remembered how they'd been unable to understand or console one another after the fire. Then she remembered that dreadful final afternoon she'd spent with him—the long years of bitter loneliness . . . and Joe.

"It was bad enough the first go-round," Lacy said. "I—I couldn't bear to relive all that again."

"I'm not asking you to." Dr. Lescuer's beeper went off, and she pushed a button to make it stop.

"If you need to go—" Lacy began in a rush.

"No—" Innocence stared directly into Lacy's eyes. "You could help him more than anyone else."

Lacy glanced past Innocence. "He's not really my concern. I've already stayed too long."

"I know I'm pushing, but Mr. Midnight is my first patient since...someone very close to me..." Innocence stopped herself. "I just don't want to lose Johnny Midnight. Look, until you came, most of the time, his eyes were dead and lost, like no one was home."

"Well they're alive now and filled with hostile dislike—for me."

"But they're not dead. Believe me, Mrs. Douglas, it must be a great thing...to feel...alive...again after having gone through what he's gone through. You have given him life."

Not wanting to hear, Lacy got up and went to the window. Distractedly, she watched a streetcar crawl up a wide street many stories below.

The real world might seem a long way away. San Francisco was down there, teeming and throbbing like a living dangerous presence in the night. But Cole was probably out there somewhere, hiding, waiting, still determined to kill her. Determined to kill Joe, too, and maybe Johnny.

She remembered the ominous car with the tinted windows that had followed her and Joe when they'd taken a limousine to the airport. She'd told the chauffeur to shake it, and he had. Then the call had come, an hour after Midnight had arrived at the hospital. Afraid he was dying, she'd rushed to him.

She hadn't intended to stay so long, but Johnny had been so terribly injured, she couldn't leave him. The weeks had drifted by, and she'd decided she needed to move from her hotel. Colleen had offered to reopen the Douglas mansion so she and Joe could move in. But Lacy had chosen to move into J.K.'s empty maid's quarters on the lower floor of his house on Telegraph Hill because they were smaller and she felt safer since J.K. was there. And he'd hired a bodyguard, Bourne, to protect them when he wasn't. She'd even enrolled Joe in the same school J.K.'s daughter, Heather, attended. She'd made friends with J.K.'s girlfriend, Honey, and her stepson, Mario. She'd begun to feel that she almost belonged on Telegraph Hill in San Francisco, and so had Joe, who didn't usually take to new people and new places.

It was a dangerous feeling—belonging—when you really didn't. When the real world was out there, waiting. No matter how she might dream, her other problems weren't going to vanish. Not that she'd been aware lately that anyone was stalking her, the way she had been aware right after Sam's death.

Yet Colleen and J.K. had warned her that as long as Cole was free, he would never give up. The police disagreed and had refused to protect her.

There was no way she could stay.

Lacy's hands splayed against the cold glass.

"Now that I know Johnny's going to get better, I have to get out of this town."

Innocence got up and joined her. "It looks like a big city out there, a big world." There was pain in her soft voice, a sad glow in her brown eyes. "You can't hide, Lacy. And you can't run, either."

Lacy swallowed. "I—I can try."

"The wrong choices hurt forever."

"That's why I'm not making any more of them." Lacy grabbed her purse and bolted for the door. "Take care of Johnny for me, will you. That's your job! Not mine!"

Innocence's beeper went off again and she impatiently pushed a button to silence it. "Mr. Midnight's very lucky because, despite the gravity of his injuries, he's sustained no visible brain damage. I see people all the time who have to learn to crawl before they can walk again, who have to relearn to tie their shoes, to knot a necktie, to feed and dress themselves. He's going to be fine. And very soon—much sooner if you stay."

"Look, I'm glad. Really glad. But—"

"I've got something else to tell you, something that I can't put in his chart, something I haven't told anyone."

"There's nothing you could possibly say to convince—"

"Then it won't hurt you to listen." There was a pause. "Before Mr. Midnight regained consciousness, he called your name—over and over again. He kept struggling to say something. He said Sam told him you were in trouble."

"Sam?" At the sound of her dead husband's name, Lacy went very white. "Are . . . are you sure he said Sam?"

"Quite sure."

"No . . ." Lacy's breathy voice was quick, panicky. "You have to be mistaken. Sam's dead!"

"That only makes what I have to say all the more important, Mrs. Douglas."

"He's dead, do you hear me?" Lacy felt sick suddenly, dizzy. Crazy nightmarish images spun in her mind. She saw Sam's blood seeping under her bedroom door. She saw the snub-nosed barrel of the .38 smashing Sam's window.

"Sam was murdered," she said in a low, terrified voice. "His killer is after me."

"He said Sam. Mr. Midnight repeated himself several times. He said Sam told him you were running for your life. Johnny said the only reason he came back through the fiery tunnel was to save you."

Lacy slumped against the door. Her voice was a slurred whisper. "Tunnel?"

"I don't have any doctor words to make this sound like it's a perfectly normal occurrence, but other patients have told me similar stories. Literally thousands of equally inexplicable near-death experiences have been documented."

"What do you mean?"

"It's really very simple. I think your Johnny may have had a near-death experience. He's forgotten it now—he was out of his mind when he told me—but I think you're the only reason he's put up such a tremendous fight these last two months to live."

Lacy spoke slowly as if her words were dragged out of her. "Surely you, a board-certified neurosurgeon, don't take hocus-pocus baloney like this seriously."

"I take anything that can affect the welfare of my patients seriously. I'm not saying I believe he really died—"

Something in Lacy's mind froze, and it was as if she were in some dark netherworld and a thin veil separated her from reality.

"Deep down in his subconscious, Mr. Midnight believes he came back from the gates of death for you, Mrs. Douglas. If you leave, he may give up. I believe that you, and only you, can make a big difference in his recovery. Especially now when he's so unsure of himself."

"He was never unsure a day in his life. That's why we broke up."

"Maybe he's always been more vulnerable than you realized."

"I came to tell him goodbye."

"You came for more than that, or you wouldn't have stayed so long."

"No—" But Lacy was suddenly finding it hard to breathe. She twisted the doorknob, frantic to escape.

"If you stay, I'll work very closely with you. You'll help with decisions—"

"I've got to go. I'm going." Lacy's voice wavered as she opened the door. "See, I'm going. I'm leaving. Now! And I—I won't be back."

"I'll let you untie him." Innocence went a step further. "I'll take Olga off the case."

Not wanting to hear more, Lacy covered both ears and ran down the hall, her hollow footsteps reverberating against the smooth white walls as loudly as her frantic heartbeat. She reached the bank of elevators and banged her hand against the black buttons.

Both elevators were stalled several floors above her.

She hit both buttons on the panel, but the elevators didn't budge.

Too impatient to wait, she raced down the stairs.

She was running from Johnny, for her life. But most of all she was running from herself.

She got as far as the main entrance of the hospital.

The night shift was coming on duty.

Olga Martinez was marching up the granite steps.

Six

Midnight awakened in the semidarkened room, terrified when hesitant footsteps paused outside his door. Hinges creaked and he strained against the straps that bound him. The crack beneath the door brightened and he held his breath, afraid it was Olga—back to exact her revenge.

Then he caught the fragrant scent of sunshine and roses and saw silver glint off silky hair. His heart pumped against the tight, hot skin that stretched across his chest.

Lacy was slim and glamorous and voluptuously beautiful. His hunger made him know that he'd once found overwhelming physical satisfaction with her—more than that. He'd loved her as tenderly as ever a man loved any woman.

Here was an even crueler and more dangerous kind of torture.

He would have bolted and run, but his lean, muscular body was staked down to his bed like a prisoner's. Completely at her mercy.

She could do whatever she wanted and he was powerless to stop her.

The muscles in his arms and legs bunched anyway.

"Don't be afraid. It's only me," she whispered, even though her violet eyes were big and terrified too.

"I'm not afraid of you," he growled.

Liar.

Too petrified to move, she simply stared—no doubt in pity.

"I was hoping you'd cleared out," he muttered ferociously.

"Dr. Lescuer bullied me into staying."

His gaze darkened moodily. "Damn her. Then I'll have to bully you into going."

Lacy looked torn. "Maybe I've decided to make up my own mind."

"Which means?"

"I'll stay—if you ask me to."

"Then you're history. Get out."

He watched warily, not wanting her to sense his fear, as she picked up a pillow and nervously plumped the downy cotton-covered rectangle.

"Damn it, I said—"

"Before I go, Johnny, you should know that Dr. Lescuer told me I could make certain decisions about your treatment."

"The last thing I want is you running my case."

Relief washed Lacy's face. She dropped the pillow. "Fine. I—I still have to say that if I stayed, I'd untie you because I don't believe you're dangerous, the way the staff says. Dr. Lescuer disagrees, but she's willing to give me a chance."

She was blackmailing him. Which enraged him.

He strained furiously against the heavy leather straps and buckles until they cut into his wrists and ankles. "Get out!"

He yelled so loudly, she jumped and then skittered hurriedly toward the door without so much as another word.

Lacy was walking out the door. Leaving him to Olga.

He felt a flicker of fear as he eyed the pillow.

"Couldn't you untie me . . . before you go?" he rasped.

But the door had closed behind her.

When he heard her soft retreating footsteps, he broke down and yelled. "Lacy!"

But she was gone.

Moonlight shone eerily on the pillow. He shut his eyes and collapsed, exhausted. He'd been a stupid, self-destructive fool not to take help from any quarter, even an enemy's.

"Yes?" came her soft, uncertain voice, breaking into his bitter despair.

Coal black eyes snapped open. "I was hoping you'd gone," he grumbled more grumpily than before.

"Did you call or not?"

"I—I suppose you could untie me . . . before you go."

"I'd be doing you a favor if I did that, wouldn't I?" But she shut the door and came closer.

"Sort of."

"A please would be nice."

"What?" Damn her. He was seized by a sudden fit of coughing that hurt him everywhere. It maddened him to be in her power.

She moved closer to him. Wisps of silvery hair had come out of the golden clip at her nape and surrounded her lovely face like gossamer silk. Her eyes were very bright as she leaned over him to unbuckle the strap that bound his left wrist. "You are so stubborn you always stick to any stand— even when it nearly kills you. J.K. says that flaw is what makes you such a good lawyer."

J.K. should keep his damned mouth shut. So should she.

But her perfume made Midnight feel hot and weak. She probably knew how beautiful she was, how much her slim, golden beauty taunted him, how desperately she made him want to be strong and whole again.

The buckle snapped loose, and she massaged the dark bruise that circled his wrist, her thumbs moving in slow circular motions that were hypnotically sensuous across his suddenly hot skin.

He lay still, scarcely daring to draw a breath because he was so tempted to grab her with his free hand, to make her know that he could still be dangerous, that he was still a man, that he wasn't so weak that he would grovel and beg her to stay once he was free.

Through half-closed lids he studied her moist, luscious mouth, her slender throat, noting that her pulse had quickened at its base as she massaged him. He despised himself for the hunger her supple fingers aroused, for the fierce surge of pulsating, quickening male need.

"Undo my other hand," he hissed through clenched teeth.

"Only if you promise to be good."

When he made a low snarl, she jumped a safe distance away from his bed. Afraid again, she stood her ground.

Damn. He stared stubbornly past her out the window.

She didn't budge.

"I promise," he thundered angrily at last.

Which seemed to satisfy her because she moved around the foot of his bed into the moonlight. But when she touched him again in that gentle way of hers that made his skin crawl with hot nerves, that made him want so much more, he realized that her hands were trembling now as if she were no more unmoved by the process than he. Her big eyes were so drastically dilated that only a ring of violet encircled her enormous black pupils.

He had to do something and soon to get rid of her, or he'd be lost.

She bit her lips as she fumbled with the shiny buckle, and he recalled that was a habit of hers when she was under stress. He realized that she really was scared of him, that she really wasn't at all sure what he'd do when she finished.

Then the buckle snapped loose, and he jerked his arm free.

Her wide terrified eyes stared into his.

He had her right where he wanted her.

She tried to run, but he grabbed her and pulled her against his chest in spite of the pain to his broken ribs.

He'd intended to hurt her, to scare her so badly she'd run away and never come back, to humiliate her as her very presence humiliated him, but when she fell against his broken ribs the ice pick in his brain gouged into a new hunk of tender tissue. Pain splintered through him. He blanched, groaning, rolling back on his pillow, panting—sweating. He was coldly furious at himself and at her, ashamed for making her so aware of his weakness.

He expected her to despise him or at least to run the second she was free.

But she leaned closer and stroked his damp brow. "Oh, Johnny—" she murmured in a low tone that was endlessly comforting. "We've both hurt each other so terribly, the last thing I ever wanted was to hurt you again."

He turned his face away, but not before he'd seen her chalky lips and her bloodless cheeks. Not before her fear and concern for him made it impossible to be as brutal as he'd intended. Then he knew he was truly lost, that no matter how stubbornly he might want to hate her, he could never hurt so much as a hair on her silvery blond head.

She looked like a woman who was having tumultuous second thoughts of her own. But she touched his chin and turned his head slowly to hers. Too shaken to speak, she lifted her tear-filled gaze and met his. With a trembling fist, her other hand clutched his hospital gown. "I shouldn't have come."

"Slim," he said softly. "It was my fault. I hurt myself. I'm all right."

"I shouldn't have untied you," she whispered brokenly. "I'll go now...."

"No—"

When she struggled he gently forced her down against his chest, his hands caressing her tense shoulders, his fingers kneading the tight muscles in her back, until she finally relaxed and curled softly next to his body like a tiny, frightened kitten to be comforted.

"I'll be good," he murmured in a low, contrite tone.

Reluctantly her arms circled his neck and she nestled her head against his warm throat for a long moment before she remembered that was the last thing she should do.

She started to pull away again, but he clasped her around the waist when she sat up.

Tears glimmered on her lashes. "I shouldn't have come back."

Ah, how right she was, but, ah, how she tempted him.

"We're so wrong for each other," she murmured.

"Right." But his voice roughened and he yanked the golden clasp out of her hair so that it cascaded over his shoulders. "You seem to have caught me in a weak moment." He slid his brown hands through the soft flowing silver, reveling in its perfumed silky texture, knowing that more than anything he wanted to go on holding her in his arms.

He needed to touch and be touched, to love and be loved. And he knew in his bones that it had been a long, long time since he'd had a woman. Just as he knew that the only woman who had ever been right for him was the one woman who was all wrong for him.

Maybe it was a blessing that he couldn't remember why he'd hated her. A God-given reprieve of some sort. She made him feel alive. The pleasure of looking at her and touching her went soul deep. She made his brain spin faster. She made chaotic fragments come together and fill the black spaces in his mind.

And she felt good, so good. His fingers skimmed the slender column of her throat, caressed her nape. Her skin was rose-petal soft and as warm as spring sunshine. Letting her stay was risky. But he needed to get on with his life, and to do that he needed to remember his past. She set things off inside him as nothing else had in the past two months.

He brought his lips to the hollow of her throat and tasted her warm skin, which was both tart and sweet like expensive champagne.

"Don't, Johnny," she protested.

But he kissed her again, and she moaned.

When he didn't stop she tipped her chin back, arched her long neck, so that her hair spilled over her shoulders like a silver veil, inviting him to do more. He reached up with both hands and traced the slender column of her neck. She moaned a second time and her flesh grew soft and pliant to his touch, her limbs boneless. A thousand sensations assaulted his body as his big hands moved lower, over white silk, erotically molding that thin, cool fabric to her warm breasts, liking it too much when she shivered.

He'd done this before. Many times. Until they'd been mad for each other. God, he'd loved her so much.

She touched him too, her frightened fingertips moving hesitantly over the rippling, hard muscles of his torso and shoulders, trying to evoke the same intense pleasure his stroking caresses were giving her. Tenderly she ran her hands beneath his strong jaw. Then she traced the tiny cuts on his dark brow.

With the back of his hands, he felt her nipples budding against creamy white silk.

"Were you always this hot?" he whispered.

Whitening, she bit her lip. "Only with you." A hoarse sob rose from deep inside her. "Not that you believed that."

Why then did he believe it now?

She seemed to stop breathing as she remembered that ancient pain. "Dear God! What am I doing? I can't let you start over on me, Johnny Midnight."

His own throat was tight. He was equally afraid. He swallowed, but it didn't help.

"Johnny, you don't remember, but I do."

"Which gives you the advantage."

"No..."

The desperate passion that blazed in her eyes jolted through him. Despite his injuries, she made him feel vitally masculine—a man again, no longer quite so afraid of his future—and totally aroused.

A wild jungle beat throbbed in his veins as her fearful, caressing gaze both defied and seduced him. Passionate conflicting emotions engulfed him, too. But when she looked at him with those heated amethyst eyes, he didn't give a damn what she'd done.

"Stay," he whispered, his voice low and charged.

"I was hoping you'd make it easy and send me away."

"What I feel isn't easy."

She nodded hopelessly. "All right... But just till you're stronger. Then we part—for good."

He was so overcome by hellish gratitude that he cried. He swallowed hard to regain control, but it was no use. More tears welled up in him. He choked. Blindly mortified, his humiliation total, he turned away to hide his ravaged face.

But she moved closer and softly kissed his brow. Then his tears, until they were gone. Placing her arms around him, she pulled him close. "It's okay. There's nobody here to see but me. And I won't tell."

She was the only one who mattered.

He sat up, his arms like iron bands around her slender frame as he clutched her and buried his face against her chest. The last thing he wanted to reveal to her was his weakness, his fears. But two months of terror boiled out of him.

"Oh, Lacy, it's been hell here—not knowing, not remembering. Sometimes I wish I'd died."

"No..." Her hands gently, tenderly massaged his neck.

"Sometimes I feel like I'm losing my mind, that I'll never be right again."

Her lovely face had gone soft with compassion. First her hands were caressing him, and then her lips in between his tortured outpourings as he tried again to tell her what had happened to him, how he was a coward. He told her about Olga, what she had done, how she had called him a vegetable, almost hypnotizing him into believing he was one.

A fierce, violent urge toward Olga rose in her. "You're not a coward. And if it's the last thing I do, I'll have that sadistic fiend fired—"

Lacy put her hand up to his face and pressed her cheek to his tenderly. Perhaps she meant only to touch her lips to his that last time. But when he opened his mouth, she kissed him hotly with the fierce ardor of one who had been starved for him for years. Her fingers wound around his neck, and she clung, seeking some closeness that went beyond sensuality.

A long time later, she drew back, her violet eyes huge and afraid. "Johnny, we can't... I—I can't... This must not happen again."

"Right."

"I'd better go now, so you can rest."

He hated the way she was so anxious to leave him.

He held onto her hand. "Before you go, tell me why we broke up."

She bit her bottom lip. The moonlight bleached her pale face. Her voice shook. "Circumstances set us against each other, but the final blow fell when I married another man."

"Why?"

"You thought you knew why." Her low tone was tight and bitter.

"Tell me."

"It's too complicated, and it's too late. Maybe I was wrong, but so were you. And I paid as dearly as you." She tried to shrug and act nonchalant, but there was a bitter intensity to her every gesture. "Please, Johnny, it's over. I can't talk about us—ever." She tilted her head back and he saw agony and sorrow and fierce anger in her too-bright eyes. "Dear God, I hate to remember."

Midnight wanted his life back, to know everything—the good and the bad. But more than that he wanted to keep her with him at least a little while longer. "Tell me about something else then."

He fitted his palm against hers very slowly. She was burning hot. A torrent of unwanted excitement moved piercingly through him. His brown fingers were more than an inch longer than her slim white ones. She watched, hypnotized, horrified by her pleasure as he laced his fingers through hers—in the old way. Then she seemed suddenly to realize what she'd let him do and pulled her hand away.

Her lip trembled, and he saw that there were tears in her eyes again. "We must not touch each other."

"Whatever you say," he agreed smoothly.

"Do you remember," she began softly, "that when you were a little boy you were afraid of the dark?"

"Did we know each other then?"

"No, you were a large boy when I first got to know you."

"Large? Do you mean fat?"

Her quick, delicious giggle triggered a memory. He'd been nineteen. She'd made that same sound from their shared fire escape when she'd crouched mischievously outside his bedroom window at his parents' house and spied on him while he'd lain sprawled across his bed, thumbing through a girlie magazine instead of his calculus text. He'd been estimating the exact measurements of a topless, busty blonde when Slim had come up behind him and giggled. He'd blushed like a kid, and she'd snatched the magazine and sprinted up the fire escape to the roof with it. When he'd recovered, he'd run after her.

With an effort he tried to force his mind from the pleasant interlude that had followed on the roof.

"You had a brother you loved very much who died—" she was saying.

He was remembering how hot he'd been for her as she'd shouted out the lascivious titles from the table of contents of his magazine while he'd chased her up the fire escape.

"Nathan," she said in a low, mesmerizing voice.

Midnight was remembering how she'd torn pictures of naked girls out of his magazine and tossed them from the rooftop—till he'd caught her to him.

"Tell me about Nathan, then," he murmured, smiling gently.

He asked more questions, and she answered—as long as he steered clear of their former relationship.

When he pressured her again the next afternoon, and the next, she grew more guarded and threatened not to visit him any more, so he stopped. But the memories she dreaded him remembering came back to him anyway.

Because someone else wanted to rekindle the pain and fury that had obsessed him and made him hate her enough to drive her away.

Someone who started sending him long white envelopes by special courier.

Seven

"Who the hell..."

Midnight tapped the long envelope against his brown palm, his fierce countenance portending violence toward the new mysterious enemy who was set on making him hate Lacy all over again by rekindling all his old most-hated memories.

As he studied the discolored newspaper clippings that lay on the table beside him, he almost preferred amnesia to what he knew and felt now.

Lacy had betrayed him and married Sam Douglas.

But before that final act she'd turned from him and embraced the Douglases and the life-style Sam could give her and he couldn't. Midnight knew that that alone had once been enough to damn her in his eyes.

The envelope in his tanned hand was just an ordinary envelope—like the others. He held it up to the light and studied the neatly blocked letters that spelled his name. It didn't look the least bit ominous, but Midnight's eyes were hard as he considered what was inside it. His hand shook as he replaced the jaggedly torn clippings and folded the white flap back down.

Hurriedly he dragged his briefcase onto his bed and unsnapped the locks. Then he lifted out the bundle of similar unmarked envelopes, studied them for a long moment before he slid this latest under the rubber band that bound the thick pack together. Quickly he relocked his briefcase.

Lacy didn't want him remembering their past. And no wonder.

But Midnight had a secret pen pal who did.

The clipping today had been of the famous newspaper picture of Sam comforting Lacy after the fire—the photograph that had been at the beginning of everything to go wrong.

Grimly Midnight stuffed the briefcase that contained the secret correspondence into his closet and kicked the door shut. Somehow he had to get his mind off that picture, off the other pictures and news stories about the fire as well— before Lacy came. She was due in less than an hour.

He looked up at the calendar above his head. Every square had been slashed by a huge X. All but one. Tomorrow's empty square was circled boldly in red.

J.K.'s postcard from Hawaii was lying on the counter under the calendar. Midnight picked it up and reread J.K.'s jubilant note for the third time. Frowning, Midnight wadded up the card and pitched it toward the trash can, swearing loudly when the crumpled ball missed and rolled toward the window. Midnight knew he should be happy for J.K., but his own mood was too bleak.

Midnight's eyes darkened as he strode to the window and picked up the postcard. He uncurled it and held it for a long moment, staring at the swirling black scrawl. Odd, how hard it was to imagine J.K. settled and happily married, how difficult to imagine him forgiving and loving.

Midnight looked across the bay. He wished he'd been well enough to have gone to their wedding. Lacy had told him the bride had worn green, and that the groom's bow tie and cummerbund had matched.

The rehab hospital was designed to look like a resort, with views and patios and fountains. The nurses didn't wear uniforms. Each patient had his own efficiency apartment. But the place still smelled and felt like a hospital, and Midnight still felt caged in, not quite himself, not in control.

Edgy.

Maybe because Lacy was coming—for the last time. Or maybe because the latest envelope had gotten to him more than he cared to admit.

He hadn't liked seeing Lacy in Sam Douglas's arms, even in that faded, yellowed clipping. He hadn't liked remembering the way Sam had used the press and an impressionable young girl, and manipulated the tragic fire to his own personal and political advantage, the way Sam had won her with his money.

But Midnight's fury mingled with prickles of uneasiness. Who the hell kept sending those clippings and cryptic messages? Who the hell was so set on him remembering everything Lacy wanted him to forget? Why would anybody give a damn?

The correspondence seemed sinister somehow. He thought of the way Lacy's eyes sometimes widened with fear, and he wished he were stronger. He wished his mind worked faster.

Was she in some kind of danger? Or was his pen-pal weirdo warning him away from her? Since she refused to confide in him and Midnight hadn't confided in her, all he could do was wonder.

Midnight glanced toward the red circle on his calendar.

Tomorrow he was going home.

But alone.

After today Lacy never intended to see him again. Midnight's hand shook as he ran it through his short black hair. Hell, why should that bother him? Their relationship had gone wrong years ago. But after a month of her sweetness he'd grown susceptible to it. He wanted more of it. He wanted it to deepen. He wanted her with him all the time, to wake up every morning and find her beside him, to lose himself in her body, to make her love him again.

Getting home, going back to work, even on a restricted schedule—these were goals he'd been busting a gut for. Now, all he felt was an insidious darkening dread.

When he'd first told her he was getting out, she'd acted thrilled. Then he'd figured out she was happy because that meant she could leave San Francisco and him—for good. He'd had to work very hard this past week to pretend he didn't give a damn, either. Not that his pride would allow him to break down when she came.

She'd served her purpose, hadn't she? Even though she wouldn't talk, his mysterious pen pal had jarred loose a lot more memories than she suspected. Memories of how the newspapers had romanticized the story into a fairy tale in which the glamorous widowed senator lavished kindnesses upon the poor grief-stricken orphan who was attending Stanford on a scholarship. How the stories said the senator's interest had gradually deepened into something else.

Until Sam, she'd seen Midnight as her prince.

And how that had hurt—not to be her hero.

Midnight tossed the postcard toward the trash and missed again. *Damn.*

He looked up at the calendar and swallowed, remembering the past month. Maybe Lacy was guilty for the past, but she'd given him new, unsullied memories he would cherish forever.

If she were as cheap and shallow as he'd believed her to be, would she have devoted herself to a convalescing man who'd once hurt her terribly, too? Her daily visits had broken the monotony of his long days. They'd been the one thing he looked forward to.

He'd spent his mornings in physical therapy and in sessions to sharpen his memory. But it was his afternoons with her that had seemed golden. She had wheeled him about the grounds until his cast had come off. Then they'd walked and talked—she, chattering when he was quiet, and listening when he wanted to talk. She'd been so good about repeating things when he'd found it hard to concentrate. She'd sweetly coached him when he'd been slow to remember something she'd told him before. Not that she ever let their new relationship go past her boundaries. She'd held herself aloof from his touch or any mention of their painful past.

But the mysterious envelopes had come every day, and the clippings and snapshots had brought back the terrible memories. Thus, despite her obstinate silence, his head was clearing and working faster. Sometimes all she had to do was look at him in a certain way to jog a memory. Sometimes one of his pen pal's cryptic notes caused troubling images to take shape in his mind. Other times the bits and scrambled fragments seemed to come from nowhere. Sometimes it took him days to assemble them into their appropriate order.

There were still gaps, but he had pieced together the vivid horrors of the fire, of Lacy's father's body being carted out along with Camella Douglas's. He had relived his own father's terrible burn injuries and long hospitalization and the clouds of suspicion that had blackened his name. Midnight recalled how he'd resented the way the newspapers had run photographs of Lacy in her stylish new clothes and made much of her easy adaption to the Douglases' lavish life-style. He remembered as well how he'd disapproved of the way she'd become almost a part of their family after she'd befriended the deeply disturbed twelve-year-old Colleen. The newspapers had noted that young as she was, Lacy had quickly learned during her years at Stanford how to manage a big house and Sam's difficult daughter, and thereby make life smoother for the bereaved senator who was away in Washington much of the time.

Midnight remembered his own bitter struggles during those years, how he'd nearly quit law school for good, how his romance with Lacy had disintegrated as she'd allied herself more and more with the Douglases, how it had finally come to an end the night his father had died and he'd shown up at the Douglas Christmas party and accused Sam of the murders. Sam had had him thrown out, and Lacy had just stood there beside Sam and watched.

Two days ago an envelope containing a blood-spotted clipping of Cole's escape from the sanitarium had been left at the nurse's station. Yesterday Midnight had received another, which dealt with Sam's murder and funeral and the reading of the will. Apparently Cole was wanted for questioning and all of Douglas's assets were frozen pending some sort of investigation. Lacy didn't have a dime she could call her own. Which was why J.K. said he'd taken her in.

Sam's murder cast the whole sorry business in a new light, but Midnight hadn't asked Lacy about it because she seemed so scared. He was afraid that if he pried he'd destroy all he had with her, their fragile present, and she'd run.

He hadn't wanted to fall in love with her again, but it had begun as he'd lain in that semiconscious state and heard her beautiful voice singing so soothingly to him through the pain and terror-filled darkness. For ten years he had wanted to hate her, but she had haunted him. Even though she now tried to act as if she visited him out of friendship, he was certain she felt much more. He couldn't forget how she'd intervened with Olga, how she'd kissed him so passionately, how she dressed so provocatively when she came to see him, how her eyes followed him everywhere when they were together.

She wore soft silk blouses and skirts that clung to her shape and rippled against her body. She left top buttons undone so that when she leaned over him he could see the creamy swell of her breasts. She wore short skirts that showed too much shapely leg. The scent of roses clung to her golden skin and silver hair, so that even after she was gone, her fragrance still hung in the air so that it almost seemed she was there. When their eyes met, she blushed.

Every day after she left he was so aroused that he would pace for hours before he could settle down to the discipline of his dull evenings—studying law, reading newspapers and magazines and professional journals, rereading deals he'd put together for J.K. He read until the early hours of the morning because he read slower now. Then he watched television to unwind. But when he slept, vague and shadowy memories taunted him from the fringes of his consciousness. He wanted to force Lacy to level with him before it was too late. Dr. Lescuer said he was pushing himself and Lacy too hard, that he would remember everything in good time.

"But Lacy will be gone by then," he had persisted.

"She stayed when you needed her the most."

"What about her needs? She's scared. Why?"

"You are too stubborn. You must respect her decision not to tell you. Relax. All that matters is you're getting well—faster than any patient I've ever had. You and Lacy have separate lives now."

"You're wrong, Innocence. Maybe getting well isn't enough. Maybe I want Lacy, too."

J.K. refused to help. "The last time I defended her, you drove over a cliff. I'm damned if I'll interfere again."

"Is the truth so terrible?"

"You used to think so."

"Did you?"

"No. But like I said, because I didn't think the truth so terrible—you damned near died. No woman's worth your life."

"She is—to me."

Eight

Lacy was never late.

Wrong. She was today. Maybe she dreaded this final visit as much as Midnight craved it. And who would blame her, Midnight thought with a pang. Maybe he was better—but he was hardly the tower of manly strength he'd once been. She had always been into fairy-tale heroes and princes—not some poor jerk who'd smashed himself up in a car wreck.

Steady. He had to play it cool for just a few more hours.

Midnight was at the mirror parting his black hair with a wet black comb as he waited impatiently for her to show. He still wasn't used to the gaunt stranger with the short haircut—all that was left of the cockily vivacious, mischievous Johnny Midnight. It wasn't just the weight loss, nor the faint scars on his tanned brow and the longer one on his right cheek, nor his closely clipped hair that bothered him. It was the deeper wounds that might hurt forever if he let Lacy walk out of his life again.

Outside he heard a tentative footstep. He watched his door with alert eyes.

When tiny white fingers curled around the huge door—at a lower level than Lacy's would have, Midnight's dark face broke into a gentle smile. He set the comb down and sank to his knees as his eight-year-old next-door neighbor shyly entered the room carrying her socks and sneakers and a big red teddy bear. When she saw him, she lost her cautious shyness and raced into his arms.

Amelia's closely cropped golden curls were a bit longer than his hair—because the shooting accident that had left the right side of her face slightly paralyzed had occurred several months prior to his.

She held up her shoes, silently smiling because this was a beloved ritual they shared every morning. He lifted her very carefully, shoes, teddy bear and all and carried her to his bed.

She bounced up and down on one foot—a new accomplishment she'd acquired this week on the trampoline in physical therapy.

"Now I know you can do your socks by yourself," he murmured, reminding her of the task at hand.

She smiled triumphantly, charmingly in that lopsided way of hers and plopped down, struggling to tug them on. "I can put my shoes on, too. Watch me, Mr. Midnight."

He leaned closer as she fought to do so.

"It's just the laces that are so hard," she panted.

"You'll be able to do that soon," he said as he tied them very slowly, in a step-by-step method, calling loops bunny ears.

She pushed his fingers aside and tried herself, but the droopy bunny ears pulled through and tangled. She tried again and again, twisting her lip as she fought to concentrate, never losing patience at her awkwardness. "Did you see me do the first part of the knot?"

"You do that great."

"It's just the bunny ears. You do it again," she commanded.

She watched and then pushed his hand away, impatient to try again. And this time she clumsily managed to tie her shoe although her loops were so huge and bedraggled they would drag and come undone.

Nevertheless, Midnight and Amelia looked up from the messy tangle, then at each other, thrilled.

Midnight threw back his black head and laughed. Amelia's arms wound around his neck, and she kissed him on the cheek. "I think I love you, Mr. Midnight," she whispered close to his ear.

She drew back blushing shyly from her confession.

He was so touched that suddenly he was blushing, too.

"When I grow up, I want a boyfriend just like you."

I was wishing I had a little girl like you.

Midnight had to tie the second shoe because she couldn't tie it no matter how hard she tried. Just as he was finishing they heard Lacy's swift, light footsteps outside. Amelia jumped down and hid behind the door, clutching her bear close and giggling expectantly.

Lacy was speaking to a nurse and Midnight felt a tearing warmth near his heart at the sound of her quick, breathy voice. All the nurses, all the orderlies liked her and looked forward to her visits—nearly as much as he did. And not because she was the celebrated Lacy Douglas—but for herself alone.

"How is Johnny today?" she asked someone at the nurse's station.

"Something's been eatin' at him mighty hard, but Amelia went in a minute ago so it's probably okay."

So something was eating at him. It galled him that his emotions were so transparent.

His face a deliberate blank, Midnight went to the mirror and shrugged into his black leather jacket as Lacy opened the door. He picked up his Stanford class ring and slid it onto his finger.

Dropping her bear, Amelia sprang out from her hiding place, and Lacy jumped and screamed, acting appropriately terrified. Then all three of them burst out laughing.

"You little rascal," Lacy said, picking up the huge bear.

"I tied my shoe for the first time. Mr. Midnight showed me how. He shows me how every day."

Lacy smiled. "That's wonderful."

"I'd better go," Amelia said, grabbing her bear. "My Mom's coming, too, and bringing Edith." Amelia bounded into the hall and then stopped and turned back to Lacy. "Did you bring Joe?"

A profound stillness closed over Lacy.

Midnight turned away, feeling sudden jealousy at the thought of Joe.

"No... not today," Lacy whispered.

"Am I ever going to get to meet him?"

Lacy looked sick and pale. "Maybe some day..."

"You always say that."

Lacy shut the door, acutely ill at ease. Because she knew her son was last person *he* wanted to think about.

The furious thought of Sam giving her a child made Midnight fight to suppress all feeling for her. He picked up his comb and pretended to study his hairline. But the scent of roses enveloped him and he was undone. His black gaze locked with hers in his mirror. His comb hung suspended above his head.

"You're always so good with her," Lacy said.

"I like kids." He hesitated. "Most kids, anyway. She's been an inspiration to me. Her injuries were so much worse than mine, and her prognosis isn't nearly as good. But she never quits—even when something's tough for her. Dr. Lescuer says she's incredible, that there's no telling how she'll be in a year—maybe she'll be almost well."

"She's adorable," Lacy said.

So are you.

Sam had gotten to touch her, to have her. For ten years. He'd given her his child. Midnight's fists tightened—those thoughts were enough to drive him mad. But as he looked at her in his mirror, his fierce longing overpowered his jealousy.

Sam was dead.

But Midnight was alive. Even if she wouldn't let him touch her, she couldn't stop him from looking at her.

Clear sun-kissed skin with more color in it now, silver hair, long-lashed violet eyes, lush curves covered in soft lavender silk. His glance devoured her as she moved, and the clinging silk shimmered in the light. He caught more of her tantalizing scent. As always the top button of her blouse was undone.

"You don't look so bad yourself," came her soft, choked voice.

He turned, so he could have a look at the real thing. She colored and looked down at her toes, but not before he'd seen an identical sting of fierce, painful need, which made his own proud, bitter heart pound.

"In fact, you look wonderful," she murmured shyly, almost daring to gaze at him again.

When he started forward, toward her, she lowered her eyes again, that one quick gesture reminding him that he could do none of the things he wanted to, things she'd let Sam do—like clasping her tightly and burying his face in her sweetly scented silver hair or savoring the exquisite sensation of her warm body melting against his.

"I don't look so hot," he muttered angrily, tossing his comb down and staring at his stiff reflection again in the mirror. "Hey, can you believe you used to think I was a hero?" His mouth twisted. "Some hero."

"I quit believing in heroes a long time ago."

Because I failed you.

She was silent.

So was he.

"Johnny—you look good. Mirrors just catch the surface stuff."

"And what do you see the mirror can't?"

She dragged her eyes slowly up the long length of his muscular torso without thinking how provocative he might find such a look. She tried to make her voice light, casual, and that maddened him more than anything she could have done.

"I see a man who can stand again, who can walk without crutches, a man who's worked very hard to relearn a lot of stuff he used to take for granted, a man who's been sweet to a little girl—a kind, brave, determined man."

"If I'm so damned attractive, why are you so anxious to get away from me and go on with your own life?"

She closed her eyes and backed toward the door. "Don't."

For God's sake stop, Midnight.

No way could he stop. Not when he wanted her more than life itself.

"Right. We can't break your precious rules."

"Johnny, I left J.K.'s car illegally parked."

"Do you really think I give a damn about J.K.'s car?"

"If you don't want to go out driving with me—"

She started backing toward the door, but he was faster.

"I do want to go—later. Right now there's something else I want more."

"Johnny, no..."

"For a whole damned month I've been waiting for you to say Johnny, yes," he growled, grabbing fistfuls of lavender silk, as he brought her closer. Some part of him was appalled. But the other part of him, which had jealously wound tighter and tighter every time she'd come to see him and offered him so little of herself, was too out-of-control to stop.

At first she held herself rigid, but as he drew her against himself and held her, something else inside her took over. She could fight neither herself nor him for very long. He was too strong, too determined, and he remembered instinctively how to touch and play to every one of her weaknesses. His hands slid burningly against her arms, back and forth, until she shivered. They ran over her soft body, molding, shaping her to his length.

The passionate eyes she lifted to his were huge and fear rounded. "Johnny, you promised me—"

"I've been a stupid idiot to stick to that. Holding you feels right to me. I have to know how it feels to you."

"We destroyed each other once." Frantically, she jammed her fists against his broad, muscular chest, inadvertently pressing too hard against his barely mended ribs.

Hot, violent pain knifed him. He sucked in a deep, agonized breath, almost doubling over. He wanted to scream against the radiating currents, to cry out like a child.

The blood drained from his dark face and he went very still. The tiny room reeled. He was miserably ashamed that she should realize how weak he still was.

"Let me go and I'll quit," she whispered, horror and fear in her eyes.

The white line of his mouth thinned, but he tightened his grip. "If I can stand it, why does it bother you?"

"It . . . it doesn't." Her slim hand pressed harder against the tender spot.

He gasped and went stiller, whiter. When she kept her hand there, he began to shake. But his tense eyes never left hers. His violent nausea made her pale, frightened face spin in a sickening whirl. Holding on to her, he groped for the wall so he could lean against it.

Just as he was about to collapse, her hand relaxed. He threw back his head and gulped in air.

Slowly her beautiful features came back into focus. He saw that her downcast lashes were wet.

Without a word he caught her shoulders and folded her closer.

"You're so damned stubborn," she whispered brokenly. "You wouldn't let go of me, no matter how much I hurt you."

"That should tell you how I feel. You wouldn't have let up, if you didn't care for me, too."

"How many times do I have to tell you—we nearly destroyed each other?"

"I think we can do better this time." His fingers pushed the soft hair at her temples aside so that he could kiss her brow. The moment his warm mouth touched her, she began to tremble.

"You promised not to—"

He kissed her nose; her damp, feathered lashes. "And I kept to that stupid bargain. Until today, Slim." His low voice was hoarse. "Don't you think you took unfair advantage of me when you exacted that pledge?" His thumbs stroked her cheekbones. The back of his knuckles skimmed her lips. "My mind wasn't working too good back then."

"You've hated me for years."

"I was a stubborn fool," he murmured quickly, kissing her with a wild urgency that made her open her mouth to his and cling breathlessly.

"I've hated you, too."

"All that matters is now. You're sweet—adorable."

"I'm leaving tomorrow."

He caressed the soft skin of her neck, his hard, possessive mouth moving over her. "Then we'd better make the most of today."

"Johnny, it's too late."

"Are you really so sure?"

And when he kissed her again she whimpered softly, closing her eyes and letting him press her body into his. For a long moment she was still. Then she returned his kisses with a ferocity that matched his own, her hands racing over his hard body. Within seconds she was burning up with desire too.

Never had he known such enthralling pleasure. It saturated his heart and mind, growing ever hotter because she felt it, too. As he deepened his kisses she clung, sliding her fingers into his crisp black hair above his collar. Soon her entire body was charged by the same wild current of pleasure. She pressed eagerly against him. He kissed her long and lingeringly. He took her kisses and answered them, their bodies melting and flowing to the sweetness of some ancient, timeless man-woman rhythm.

He felt violent and dark with passion, and yet incredibly tender, too.

A man again. Almost whole.

His hands went beneath her, lifting her hips against his so that she knew how fully she aroused him.

She gasped and her grave face rose to his, studying him first with eyes and then with her hands. Their bodies fused, she reached up and traced his cheeks with fingertips that trembled, touching, relearning every chiseled feature.

When her hands fell away, her eyes stayed, growing so solemn and gentle his heart doubled its pace.

"Oh, Johnny, what's happening to us?" She looked so sweet and vulnerable, and so afraid.

"Something that was meant to happen," he said quietly.

He would have said more, but the phone rang. And even though he tried to hold her and persuade her to let it ring, she struggled loose and stumbled across the room to answer it.

He leaned against the door, raking his hands through his hair, watching her, almost amused when she fluffed her bangs and tried to speak normally. Then she sensed that he was looking at her and she looked away, a rosy blush staining her cheeks.

His mouth curved in a slow smile. He wanted her—everything from her. But he had to go slow. The thought panicked him because he was running out of time.

Careful not to look at him, she hung up the phone. "They're going to tow J.K.'s car if we don't get down there. They said five minutes."

He grinned almost as cockily as he would have before the accident. "Five minutes, huh?"

She fluffed her bangs again. Then she straightened her collar with an unsteady hand. Her voice was tight. "Don't even think about it."

His white grin broadened as he considered the pouting fullness of her delectable lips, which were still swollen from his kisses. "Every time I look at you, Slim, I think about *it.*"

He moved, and she jumped. He liked that, too.

"I think we should say goodbye."

"Hey, hey—you promised to take me on my first joyride. Now what kind of woman breaks a promise to a wounded man?"

She fumbled with her purse. "You broke a more important promise to me."

"We both enjoyed it."

She kept fiddling with her hair. She adjusted the strap of her purse. "That's hardly the point. You broke your promise, so I can break mine."

"But you won't—because, you're a whole lot more honorable than I am."

"You didn't used to think so," she said too quietly.

Her eyes shifted away, but not before he felt their raw, unadulterated pain.

Then he knew that he'd hurt her as terribly as she'd hurt him. Perhaps more. And because he had, she was determined to leave him—forever.

Nine

It was a cool, gray afternoon with only intermittent sunshine. A Pacific storm was predicted to hit that night, but Lacy and Midnight drove with the top down anyway.

It was his first taste of freedom after months in hospitals. He should have felt like a man set free from prison, but he didn't. Instead freedom meant only that he was losing Lacy and after that he'd have nothing more to lose.

Instead of the famous sights, he memorized the way the wind and sunshine played in her flying hair. She took him to North Beach, and he insisted on getting out so they could see the view of Alcatraz and the bay from Coit Tower and Pioneer Park, which was right above J.K.'s mansion on Telegraph Hill.

"You used to think Alcatraz was a castle," he murmured, coming close to her as she ignored him and peered through one of the telescopes. He brushed the heavy hair from her nape caressingly. "Do you remember that time I took you? How we kissed in the fog and almost missed the last boat back?''

She jumped away from his unexpected touch, her violet eyes clouding. "Your memory's coming back. You didn't tell me."

"There are a lot of things you haven't told me, either," he muttered in a tight, goaded undertone, pulling her toward him and kissing her before she stiffened and reminded him that kissing was off-limits.

"Sorry," he whispered with biting sarcasm, letting her go. When she stalked past him as if he didn't exist, he swore bitterly but followed.

He was almost surprised when she waited for him in the car.

That little scene made her tenser for a while. Silently they drove along the Embarcadero. Silently they ate bouillabaisse at Fisherman's Wharf. Afterward they roared across the Bay Bridge to Berkeley and back once more to the marina where she stopped at Marina Green and they got out. By then some of her tension was gone, and he might have enjoyed the park if only he hadn't known the shining moments of their last afternoon were slipping away as quickly as sand through an hourglass.

She sat stiffly on a blanket on the grass with all her invisible walls in place and pretended to watch teenage boys play touch football while sailboats tacked aimlessly back and forth on the glittering blue bay. He just watched her.

She'd brought sandwiches and coffee which she ate and sipped in that awful silence. She flew a kite for a while and then gave it to some children and lay down on the blanket beside him again, more relaxed.

"I love this city," she said, staring up at the darkening clouds rushing past. "When I was growing up, I wanted to escape. Do you want to know something funny? Sometimes I think I was happier back then."

"I know I was," he said too sharply.

Before we gained the world—and lost each other.

He didn't have to say it. She knew what he meant. After that she wouldn't speak to him again. He couldn't speak either.

The late afternoon sun was reddening the fringes of the black storm clouds and the buildings and backlighting the trunks and leaves of the trees. The shadows had deepened to indigo purple when she finally got up to go.

Because she shivered, he took off his black leather jacket and wrapped her in it, which made her seem sexier to him than ever. For a wondrous second as he held her close, his heart thudded. So did hers.

He knew not to touch, but his hands had a will of their own. Lifting her chin with his thumb and forefinger, he forced her lips to his again. The moment his mouth took hers, she trembled, whether with fear or desire he did not know. But her arms circled his neck and they clung for a delicious instant, as if she wanted to savor for the last time the bittersweet excitement of him, too. Then she remembered she was afraid, and tearing herself free she ran toward J.K.'s black car.

"I guess we've seen all the main sights," Lacy whispered, white-faced, not looking at him when he caught her and opened the door. "I-I'll remember today forever."

An immense black cloud moved across the sun. "Right. It was beautiful. But it's over. Thanks."

"Dreams always end, Johnny. At least mine have."

"Mine, too." He snapped the words out.

All the magic, rosy light seemed to have vanished from the day. Everything grayed. Even her lovely face. The air was suddenly colder. So was his mood.

She was heading to the hospital, holding on to the wheel as tightly as she seemed determined to hold on to her emotions when she asked in a strained voice, "Is there anywhere else you'd like to go?"

"Since you asked, Slim—"

Her gaze met his and, reading his mind, grew wide with fear.

"Where?" she mumbled, barely moving her lips, staring desperately back to the road, because she already knew.

"Why not the old neighborhood?"

"Johnny?" She went grayer.

"If you didn't want to know, you shouldn't have asked."

"That's the last place we should go. It's too dangerous."

"For whom?"

She couldn't answer.

"Not for two old-timers like us, Slim. We grew up there, remember? Oh, yeah, that's the point. The last thing you want to do is remember."

Her voice was unsteady. "Somebody'll probably try to steal J.K.'s car."

"Not a chance. Honey teaches there. He goes down there all the time. The creeps know this car. They know him."

"Then—" Her eyes were stricken. She was nibbling on her bottom lip. The ends of her hair flew about her white face like dry whips.

"Will you quit with the excuses?" He leaned across her shoulder and grabbed the wheel. When he shoved it all the way to the left, the sports car careened onto Market, skidding on two tires.

They barely missed a bus.

The driver blasted them furiously with his horn.

"Johnny!"

"Don't argue. Do you know the way, or do you want me to keep steering?"

"I know the way." Her mutinous grip tightened on the wheel.

Grimly he removed his hand and shot a glance behind them, having noticed that a little blue foreign car with a dented front bumper had made the same sudden turn they had.

Coincidence? He drew a deep breath. Maybe. But maybe not.

Ten blocks later Midnight flipped his visor down nonchalantly, so he could look in the mirror. The little blue car was still behind them, although stealthily hanging farther back. When they turned again, it turned too. Midnight cursed under his breath. He stole a tense glance at Lacy and thanked God that she hadn't noticed.

The sun had gone down and the last of the light was fading when she reached their old street.

Most of the topless bars had vanished—probably thanks to the new morality brought on by the need for safe sex—but there were more pawn shops and graffiti than he remembered. The two Queen Anne houses they had lived in had been divided into tiny apartments. Dingy curtains fluttered from the third-story windows. The fire escape looked limp and rusty. The paint was peeling off both houses. Bits of weathered gingerbread trim were missing at the roofline.

"Stop the car," he commanded.

"Why?"

"Because I want to get out and take a stroll down memory lane."

"Johnny—"

"Hey. Am I touching you? Am I asking personal questions? Am I breaking any of your damned precious rules?"

"I didn't want to come here," she murmured weakly.

"Then let me out and leave."

"I can't do that."

"Then you've got a problem, Slim."

When she pulled up in front of her old house, she wouldn't look at it. Two boys were throwing a football in the middle of the dark, shadowy street. She hunched forward like a wounded animal, shut her eyes and buried her face in her hands.

Why the hell was he torturing her by stubbornly pushing for his own way like he always did? Hell, why was he tor-

turing himself? Midnight balled his hands into fists. Then he unflexed them and nudged her shoulder gently.

The instant his tense fingers grazed her arm she jumped away, scooting closer to her door.

"Not all the memories you're running from are bad," he said gravely. The brown hand that she cringed away from sifted through her wind-tousled hair. "I remember the day we met. The night we first made love—" His voice had deepened. "Did you know rainy nights still turn me on? I can't ever sleep through one without thinking of you, without wanting—"

She turned then, swallowing hard, her lovely eyes raw with the most terrible pain as she studied his handsome face. "Those are the most awful memories of all."

"Not for me," he whispered. "Not any more. I want them. All of them. I want you, too. I want to make it up to you—for shutting you out. I want to forgive you."

She gave a dry, rending sob.

"Okay," he muttered furiously, withdrawing his hand. "I'll stop pushing. You can go."

"No. I'll wait here for you."

He got out of the car and called the kids over who were playing ball. He unfolded a twenty from his wallet so they could see it. "Watch the car. Keep an eye on the lady, too."

They eyed the bill and then each other, nodding with pop-eyed small-boy importance.

Midnight began to walk toward the vacant lots where the warehouse had once stood, noting the small blue sedan with the battered bumper parked at the end of a side street.

He heard Lacy's car door slam. Then he heard her light hurried footsteps beside him, and he stopped and waited.

Sam had held her here for the first time while the warehouse burned. While Midnight's father had lain unconscious and terribly injured with that incriminating lighter clutched tightly in his hand.

When Midnight saw her sudden tears, he put his hand gently over hers, lacing his fingers over hers and comforting her as once Sam had comforted her on this very spot and the news photographer had damned them all by snapping the famous picture.

The picture would have haunted Midnight even if it hadn't come in the white envelope today. Had Sam, the bastard, ever loved her? Or had he merely dazzled an impressionable young girl and used her because she had become such a sympathetic figure to the press that her pure image made the press forget the ugly rumors about Sam's first wife's death?

"I—I can't stay," Lacy whispered. "There are too many ghosts."

"For me, too." Midnight slid his thumbs across her smooth cheekbones. "We were both standing here the night our lives went wrong and Douglas damned us both to hell. Let's start over today—here—where everything went wrong. I think I can forgive the past, if we're truthful with each other from now on."

"Johnny, this isn't a child's game."

"Don't you think I know that? Sam's first wife was murdered here. So were our fathers. Mine slowly and horribly. Besides that, Sam Douglas framed him."

"Johnny, don't start in on Sam again. He was murdered too."

At her defense of Sam, he flushed angrily. "Now why would anybody want to kill a nice guy like Sam?"

"I'm not sure."

"You married the bastard. You were there when he died."

"Don't ask me about that night—"

Midnight swore silently. "Why not—unless you have something to hide?"

She looked frantically past him into the darkening shadows of the alley. "I didn't kill Sam."

Midnight saw that she was hellishly, dangerously scared. "Who did?" he asked in a softer tone.

"Cole. And I think he's after me, too. That's another reason why I've got to get out of San Francisco."

"Did you see him that night?"

"I heard his voice in the next room...at least I *think* it was him. Who else—"

"I'm not sure of a damned thing any more. There are gaps in my head—" Midnight broke off, never liking to admit that. "Until Sam died, I thought he set the fire and framed my father. I thought he used his money and influence to buy the press and squelch the investigation—to buy you and make himself look like some saint who'd married a sweet orphan. Image was everything to the Douglases. I wonder now if Sam locked up Cole for ten years to shut him up."

"Johnny, you're wrong. Sam loved Cole. He wanted to protect him. His breakdown broke Sam's heart."

"Sam Douglas never gave a damn about anybody but himself," Midnight snarled.

"Let's just drop it."

"Four people have died violently. My father was framed. I want to know why. If someone's after you, I want to stop him."

"You're too weak right now."

Damn her. Too furious to speak, Midnight clamped his teeth together.

She went on. "If you couldn't prove anything then, what makes you think you can get any closer to the truth now?"

"Because somebody's still out there killing people. If I push, sooner or later he's going to mess up. I want my life back. I lost it here—that night. I lost you, too. I want to know what really happened. But most of all I want to start over with you."

"Sam's dead."

"Which means you're free."

"Johnny, you've always believed me capable of the most hideous things. You thought I married Sam for his money. You thought I would have married him even if I'd believed he was a killer."

"Well?"

She paled.

He persisted. "Was I right? Admit it, if you did. I'd rather start over with the truth than a lie."

"You see what I mean! You're as blind as you were back then. You still think I'm that low." Her quiet, pain-filled voice continued. "You say you want the truth, but what you want is your own stubborn version of it."

"Did you marry Sam because you loved him?"

"I—I thought he cared about me. I wanted to be part of a family."

"The rich and famous Douglas family."

"They took me in when I was homeless."

"Did you marry him for love? Yes or no, Slim?"

"N-no..."

"I rest my case."

Her luminous eyes flashed. Her hand stiffened in his but he held on tightly.

"Your case!" she cried. "You pushed me into that marriage because you were stubborn and cruel. You abandoned me! Now all I want is a fresh start—alone. In the past I thought I needed a man to protect me, but you tore me apart and Sam manipulated me with his power and money. Now all I want is to learn how to protect myself. I want to be alone. Free—of you."

"Neither one of us will ever be free of the other, you little fool."

"I will! I will!" Tears spilled in earnest down her frozen face.

Midnight stared at her, cut to the marrow, too dazed for a moment to realize what was happening. How could she act like she was such an innocent? How could she reject his generous willingness to forgive her everything? To reject his offer to help her fight Sam's killer? *To reject him.*

Midnight wanted to seize her and shake her, to force her to do what he wanted. But he felt too fierce, too near some dangerous edge.

"Goodbye," she whispered, her voice utterly calm. Utterly shattering to him. "Good luck."

As if such a platitude were all he needed.

She put him in hell. He grew paler in his effort to leash his fury. He couldn't stand losing. Not his heart. His life. Her. Everything that had ever mattered.

On the other side of the bay a sliver of lightning cut across a purple sky.

Her lips touched his. Their voluptuous sting on his burning mouth was brief but devastating.

His collar seemed to tighten until he felt as if he were choking. He wanted to smash something, to tear something apart.

Her face was white and pinched as she glanced into the smoldering violence of his eyes for the last time. Then she pulled her fingers free of his and walked slowly back to the car.

The blue-black pieces of the dismantled gun lay hidden in their aircraft aluminum case halfway beneath the passenger seat.

The killer tensely lifted the scope out and peered through the cross hairs at Lacy in Midnight's too-large leather jacket as she walked up to Johnny, pushed up the long black sleeves and took his hand.

The neighborhood had gone to hell. It was worse even than it had been the night of the fire when wicked orange flames had licked the tops of the squalid buildings. Too bad it had started to rain and the fire fighters had contained the fire within a single block. Too bad the whole damned neighborhood hadn't been reduced to ashes.

The killer leaned forward. Lacy was speaking earnestly, passionately. Even to someone who hated them both, they made a handsome couple—Midnight so dark and tall and lithely powerful in spite of his recent injuries, she smaller and so gracefully slim, with her long silver hair and stylish clothes. Midnight was leaning down to catch her every word. Surely this meant Lacy and Joe would stay in San Francisco.

That was good because Johnny Midnight deserved to die for what he'd done as much as the others had. He had betrayed the family, endangered the family. He'd come too dangerously close to the truth.

And he'd loved Lacy.

Too bad he hadn't died in that wreck. Still, it had been a thrill this past month—knowing his brilliant mind was paralyzed by amnesia. A thrill stringing him along with the clippings. It would be even more thrilling to finish off the three of them together by some bizarre method that would make all the papers.

The killer smiled, imagining the sensation of that final clipping.

Then a frown chased away the triumphant smile at the sight of Lacy's intense expression. The sweet little lovers' scene was going up in smoke just as the warehouse had.

The killer began to sweat as Lacy broke free of Midnight's grip and walked away. Midnight remained where he was, impassive and still. In the dim, darkening light of the early evening, his tall form seemed even taller and more rigid. His lips were compressed as though in fury, as if only his fierce will held in check some surging passion. He took a single step after her, as if to follow, and then stopped himself as his bleak, bitter pride shut down every other emotion.

The show was over. Time to pack up and go. The loving couple had split up again.

Black kid-covered fingers replaced the scope in the aluminum case beside the gun as gently as a lover might caress a woman.

Lacy started Cameron's car and sped off.

Midnight shoved his hands in his pockets and walked away in the opposite direction, vanishing into the purpling shadows.

Not good. Midnight had to die with Lacy and Joe. This time if he didn't, he'd dig till he got to the truth.

From the way things looked, Lacy and Joe would be leaving town tomorrow after all.

Unless someone played Cupid and stopped them.

How?

The black-gloved hand shakily switched on the ignition of the blue Toyota.

Another envelope?

Too slow. And boring.

Nothing could be left to chance.

A telephone call would be more fun.

It was almost too late when the killer heard an empty beer can roll into the gutter. The sprinting footsteps less than twenty feet behind the car brought a sickening feeling of déjà vu for one panicky, heart-hammering second.

The bastard must have known he was being watched all along.

A brick shattered the rear glass window. Then Midnight lunged, and the killer screamed, stomping down on the accelerator in a maniacal rage. Midnight's body hit the trunk so hard he partially dented metal. But the car shot forward and he fell backward as the Toyota flew over the curb, bounced down the sidewalk, slammed into a fire hydrant and jounced back over the curb and onto the street. All the glass in the back windshield fell out.

Water shot everywhere, raining into the car. But soon Midnight was a small, diminishing figure in the rearview mirror beside the bright spraying geyser.

The killer was still shaking ten minutes later.

That had been close. Too close.

The damaged car would have to be repaired or dumped. Which wouldn't be easy.

The tricky bastard had to die.

Ten

Shivering and exhausted, his jaw clenched against the hot, throbbing ache above his sore ribs, Midnight limped slowly down the long hall toward his suite. He wished he'd gotten a better look at the driver of the Toyota. It had been pretty dark. All he'd seen was the back of his head.

Jumping on the trunk had been a dumb move. He was lucky as hell the jerk hadn't backed over him. He was thankful as well that he was still too numb to feel the agony of losing Lacy, even though he knew that the pain would shatter him later.

Then he saw Amelia stretching her thin body to make herself taller as she struggled to use the pay phone across from his room at the end of the hall. Her brows were screwed together in frustration. Her cheeks streaming with tears, she held several coins and the receiver in one fist and punched in numbers frantically with the other. Now why was she out in the hall when she had a phone of her own?

Midnight squeezed his eyes shut and drew a long breath. God, he hated this place. He hated a world that could do this to a little girl. It hurt him just to watch her.

Not that he was doing so great himself. He was weaker than he wanted to admit—dead tired and depressed after his failure with Lacy and the creep in the blue Toyota. The two-mile walk afterward had wiped him out. More than anything he wanted to lie down.

Her eyes wild and desperate with defeat, Amelia threw down the receiver and strangled on a sob as it banged the wall.

Something broke in him, and he went over to her and sank to his knees, taking her face in between his hands.

Eyes that were blurred with tears stared up at him. "I...don't want...you...to...see...me...cry."

"Hey, don't tell anybody, but I cry sometimes." He put his arms around her and drew her tight, stiffly jerking little body into his arms. "It's been a bad night for me, too."

"You're...not...crying...now...?"

"I wish I could."

He held her until she quit sobbing. Then he gave her a tissue to dry her face.

She was staring at the phone, wiping her eyes. "I forgot how to do it." Her small, tragic voice was slightly slurred. "My mom's using my phone. I'm stupid—too stupid... I'll never be smart again."

"Hey, hey..." he soothed. "Don't say that. Everybody forgets, Amelia." He picked her up. "Now who were you trying to call? And you'd better not make me jealous by telling me it's another guy."

She smiled through her tears and held out a scrap of paper with a phone number. "No, silly. My best friend, Edith."

"First," he began gently, enunciating every word, "you pick up the receiver."

She was listening, interested.

"I did that!"

He touched her fingers, which fiercely gripped a shiny coin. "Then you put the quarter in the biggest slot."

"Oh. I thought it was the nickel."

"Then—you dial."

Her smile was almost radiant again. "Can I do it by myself now?" she asked softly.

He ruffled her hair and put her down.

He was watching her clumsy fingers laboriously dial each number when he heard his own phone.

"That thing's been ringing off the wall for the past hour," one of the orderlies yelled from the nurse's station as Midnight pushed his door open.

It had to be Lacy. Midnight hadn't really expected her to change her mind and call him after their quarrel. But like a lovesick fool, he was so desperate he would have forgiven her anything in that moment. He despised his eagerness as he rushed for the phone. He had to fight to keep his voice steady. "Slim—"

The low chuckle against his ear made the hair on the back of Midnight's neck rise, as if an icy draft had blown in through an open window. "We both wish," came a sinister whisper. "Call me Cupid—the love god."

"Are you the jerk in the Toyota?"

"I've been writing you, too."

"Go to hell." Midnight slammed the phone down. In the next second he wished he hadn't.

It rang again.

And again.

Midnight picked it up in a panic.

"Hang up on me again, and I'll make a mess of Lacy before I kill her," came the childlike, androgynous whisper, deadlier and icier now.

"Who the hell is this?"

"I told you—Cupid, the love god. Did you know she's taking her kid with her tomorrow?"

"How long have you been following her, you sicko?"

"Her kid's the important issue here."

"No! You scumbag, you're—"

"Hasn't Lacy told you?"

Midnight's voice was hoarse and shaking. "You stay away from her! Don't even think about her!"

The whisper grew more terrible. "Joe's her kid. Your kid, too. Same kid. Do I have to spell it out? You're a daddy!"

"What the hell—"

"*D-A-D-D-Y.*"

Midnight drew a long breath.

The whisper softened. "She had morning sickness so bad on her wedding day, she could barely stumble down the aisle. She was so sick because of your kid during the reception, Sam had to cancel their honeymoon cruise. But do you blame her? Who would want a slum boy's kid? Who wouldn't want to pass the brat off as the wealthy senator's? She was smart, valedictorian of her class—a star. She got the best deal she could. You used to be a lawyer, so you ought to understand. You'd still be doing it, if you hadn't knocked your brains loose in that accident."

"You son-of-a—"

Then the line went dead.

Midnight's black eyes glazed over. His head ached. The walls of the suite seemed to breathe in and out to the same rhythm as his pulse hammered.

He felt explosive.

Like he was really going mad.

He yanked the phone out of the wall and threw it across the room.

The despair and self-loathing he felt seemed bottomless. Had Lacy really thought so little of him she'd deliberately passed his son off as Sam's?

Midnight wanted to tear the room apart. He wanted to kill. He wanted to die.

But first he had to deal with Lacy.

* * *

The night seemed hostile. The sky over distant Oakland crackled eerily with electric cobwebs as the taxi raced up and down the dark, silent streets like a jungle cat on a rampage. The traffic light at the top of the hill flashed yellow.

Midnight put his elbow on the dash and leaned toward the driver. "Ten bucks more if you run it. Two hundred if you're unlucky and get a ticket."

"The way you break laws you're either a lawyer or a cop. Since you're flashing money, I'd say lawyer 'cause they like to steal more than cops do."

Midnight flashed two green bills. "How'd you guess?"

"You meet the best classes of people in this racket."

"I meet the worst in mine."

A horn blared as they raced through the light.

Midnight left the bills on the dash and sank back against his seat and fastened his seat belt.

"High time," the driver muttered. "What happened to your face?"

"Reckless driver."

"That figures, too. Your kind lives fast. Dies fast, too."

"When we get lucky."

The cabbie snorted, but Midnight was no longer aware of him. He was wondering about Joe. Just the name made fresh fury at all of Lacy's old injustices coil through him. Was it true? Was Lacy that treacherous? All of Midnight's willingness to forgive and forget her marriage to Sam had vanished.

He remembered how carefully she'd changed the subject every time Joe's name had come up, how awkwardly she always acted about him.

What kind of woman kept such a secret from a man?

He already knew.

The kind who sold herself for money. The kind who'd tried to sell him, too—and to a man he hated—just to ease her own sorry conscience. The kind who had snuck up on his blind side, acting kind and sweet. The kind who had used his amnesia and vulnerability to get close to him so she could stick the knife in all over again. The kind who thought it was fun to wear clingy silk and tease him with undone buttons so he'd feel tight and hot and starving for her. The kind who let him kiss her and hold her just enough so he couldn't forget the tantalizing taste of her and then walk out of his life forever. Would such a woman stop at passing off his kid as a Douglas?

And yet every time he remembered the whispered conversation on the telephone and the slim black-gloved hands holding that scope, he remembered as well that four people had already died.

The guy was after Lacy. He would kill her and maybe Joe, too—if Midnight didn't stop him.

When the cabbie let him out at J.K.'s house, Midnight paid him to wait.

Despair stole the breath from Lacy's body as she set down the phone on the table next to Midnight's leather jacket. She pulled her red silk robe more tightly around her and told herself she needed to resume her packing.

Instead she stared down at the phone.

Lacy had wanted to tell Colleen goodbye before she left the States, but as usual she'd gotten Colleen's answering machine. Besides saying goodbye, Lacy had needed reassurance too—after her last dreadful farewell to Johnny.

Lacy picked up the phone and then put it down. Colleen was gone, probably preparing for that big part she'd told Lacy about at the funeral.

For an instant Lacy's fingers traced across the soft black leather jacket. Then she jerked her hand away as if stung. She still felt queasy, sick to the soul when she remembered Midnight's furious hurt as she'd freed her hand from his. Not even the knowledge that a killer was after her upset her as much as knowing she'd never see Johnny again. Why did it hurt so much to leave him when for ten years she'd told herself she hated him?

Because she'd never hated him.

She'd known that the instant she'd heard he was dying. She should have run then.

But she had stayed and nursed him until he regained consciousness. A lone tear rolled from the corner of her eye as she remembered how his strong, tall body had lain so still and helpless, how all those hideous machines and tubes had made awful gurgling noises as if they'd been more alive than he was, how she'd sat by his bed and prayed that he would wake up and be himself again.

This past month, when he'd gotten better every day, she'd thrilled to even his smallest achievement—even though being with him had been a special kind of torture because she'd felt such a powerful compulsion to touch him, to kiss him, to smile . . . to let him know how deeply she still cared. To do more. To forgive and forget. To be close.

To make love again. To share her life with him.

But she remembered too well how terribly they'd hurt each other at the end.

She buried her face in her hands and wept. How she longed for his mouth, his hands, his body. She always would, but if she'd allowed herself to surrender fully to that passion again, she would never have been able to walk away.

Listlessly she wadded up another silk blouse and stuffed it into her suitcase. *He'd begged for another chance— sweetly, passionately, and then darkly, willfully, in every way that could move a woman who was deeply in love with him.*

She thought of the way his dark, smoldering gaze had burned her, the way his strong hands had touched her and made her know that her body fitted his, the way his lips . . .

Dear God. Desire and need and poignant loss wound tighter and tighter. Why couldn't she quit tormenting herself? She knew well enough what he would think of her when he got all of his memory back.

She hadn't slept with Sam.

Or anyone else. But he wouldn't believe that.

Only Johnny—all those long, long years ago.

And how many countless nights since had she lain awake for hours staring up into the darkness, restless and lonely and starved for a man's touch? For love? And yet unable to seek it in the arms of the many masculine admirers who'd passed through her glamorous life and let her know from time to time they were available for an affair or something more.

No other man but Johnny would do.

Then why was she leaving him?

Because she had to.

Even if Johnny could forgive her for Sam and all the rest, he'd never forgive her for Joe. And Joe was too fragile now to sustain the shock of Johnny, especially a newly betrayed Johnny livid with fresh hate. She remembered how cold and remote he'd been before. This would be worse. She couldn't bear the thought of her child being torn between two warring parents. And how would Joe feel about her if he knew? She, who had known so little love, couldn't risk losing Joe's.

No, she had to put Joe first for once, to take him away where he'd be safe and unconfused, and where she could lavish him with the attention Sam had never allowed her to give. She needed to develop her own relationship with him before she tested it with another.

Then there was Cole. The police didn't want her to leave the country, but they'd never done anything to protect her. Sooner or later Cole would find her, if she didn't take Joe and run.

These well-worn rationalizations flew through her brain as she tore clothes from hangers and threw them onto the floor in heaps. Usually she was neat and organized, but tonight the maid's quarters on the bottom of J.K.'s mansion were a wreck.

Unwashed dishes littered the counter. Joe's room was worse. When she'd ordered him to clean it and pack, he'd shrugged his shoulders with that arrogant Johnnylike, Mom-you're-crowding-me indignation and stomped upstairs to watch a football game with Mario, Honey's older stepson. Nero had pricked forward his good ear and whined at her defiantly and then dashed after his young master.

Joe should have been in bed hours ago, but she was a miserable failure as a disciplinarian. Joe didn't want her affection. He didn't respect her. And why should he? She'd left Joe to the staff and his Austrian governess too much, and he was used to being waited on.

When Lacy was with Joe, she felt so guilty she usually gave in to him. She hadn't spent enough time with him since they'd been in San Francisco, because he'd been in school and she'd been visiting Johnny. But after tomorrow she would be able to devote herself to Joe full time. Not that he wanted her to, or that he wanted to go.

On the contrary, Joe was used to independence, and he liked San Francisco. He had spent a lot of time with Mario and Heather. And he didn't mind the cramped maid's quarters.

"At least I get to see you now," he had said coolly one morning, after she'd apologized for the three tiny rooms.

He didn't talk to her all that often, and that, like many of his few, well-chosen remarks, had hurt.

It hurt, too, that Joe even preferred J.K. to her and had followed him everywhere because he was so starved for masculine attention.

Joe had always wanted a father, but every outrageous stunt he'd pulled to get Sam's attention had backfired and only served to increase Sam's natural resentment of the boy who wasn't really his. Joe hadn't understood Sam's rejection, and he hadn't stopped trying to win Sam's affection.

Johnny Midnight would have made a wonderful father.
Dear God . . . She shouldn't let herself think about that.
But she did.

Johnny was wonderfully, incredibly patient with children. Lacy remembered how gentle he had been with Amelia. He had been good with the Douglas children, too. Joe, who wanted a father more than anything, would have adored Johnny. And Johnny—

It was too late now. Joe's problems were hers alone, and she would have to help him solve them all by herself.

She was slamming the lid of her suitcase when Nero started barking wildly from the loggia upstairs at someone or something on the street.

She heard brisk footsteps approaching the front door. Then the doorbell rang. Nero bounded down the stairs, growling through barred teeth.

Lightning flashed, but Lacy was afraid to lift the shade and look out.

It was nearly eleven. She wasn't expecting anyone. Bourne, her bodyguard, had taken the night off.

The doorbell buzzed loudly again, echoing up the staircase, which spiraled upward five stories to the elegant living quarters, terraces and loggia. Moonlight sifted eerily from the domed skylight at the top of the stairwell. The paintings and shadowy furniture took on ominous shapes.

When a balled fist pounded on the wooden door, Nero pranced insanely. Lacy's heart was beating like a drum. Her mouth felt dry as she backed slowly away from the door.

Nero lunged wildly at the doorknob, barking savagely. When the buzzer and knocking stopped abruptly, the Doberman settled tensely back down on his haunches and kept growling.

Joe came out to the landing and peered down. "Mom, they're about to make a touchdown. Are you going to get the door or not?"

She jumped, startled. "Uh, yes, I am. You go back to your game!"

A man's class ring furiously tapped glass. "Lacy, it's me—Johnny. Unlock the door."

Johnny—she was almost relieved.

Until she remembered Joe.

"Sit," she commanded Nero. Then she disarmed the alarm and let Johnny in. He looked good, *too* good, in tight faded jeans and a crisp white shirt.

The sky flashed and darkened. Thunder rumbled as Midnight shut the door and reset the alarm, punching in the intricate code *from memory*.

His face was gray with exhaustion. Dark shadows edged his eyes. He was running on sheer willpower. *And anger.*

Anger as cold as the anger that had spurned her ten years ago.

"Looks like rain," she whispered weakly.

"You know it never rains in San Francisco."

"Except when we're together."

Their eyes met, and she remembered another night, another lifetime.

Nero licked his fangs impatiently, and when she whispered sit again he whined, his whole body quivering reluctantly.

"He'd like to eat me alive." Midnight's gaze narrowed. "Same as you would. Bet he'll be a hell of a lot easier to tame than you." As if to prove his point, Johnny hunkered down so Nero could sniff his hand, and soon Nero was wagging his tail and begging to be petted. "What happened to your ear, fella? Did you meet a brute even meaner and uglier than you?"

Words were beyond her as she listened to that raspy drawl she loved and watched how easily he charmed her dog. Leaning weakly against the wall, she ran her tongue across her dry lips.

She had always been just as easy for him to charm—too easy.

Midnight stood up slowly. "Some watchdog." His face grew even colder.

"W-we already said goodbye," she whispered.

"Right." His voice was deeper, harsher. An ugly light flared in his black eyes as they devoured her trembling body, which was too revealingly clad in the thin silk robe. "Our goodbyes were premature." His eyes darkened as he took in the wild disarray of her blond hair and the silky texture of her pale skin.

She drew the robe about her body more tightly. "I—I was packing."

"So I see." A muscle jumped convulsively at the corner of his mouth. "There are more enjoyable ways for a beautiful woman to spend her evenings."

"I really do have important things to do."

"Don't we all?" His searing gaze licked over her with devastating thoroughness.

She wished she were wearing more—something thicker, something that didn't cling to her body. She felt hot color creep over her cheeks. "I have a plane to catch."

Ruthlessly he contradicted her. "You're not going anywhere, Slim."

"Johnny—" She glared at him mutinously.

He was staring at the bike and football and dog-eared tour guide to Alcatraz Joe had carelessly thrown down. On a low table lay a little jumble of treasures and trash—two marbles, four rocks, peanut shells and two chocolate candy wrappers.

Her blood congealed as his black gaze studied them.

"Where is he?" Midnight hissed through clenched teeth.

"What are you talking about?"

"I know about Joe."

Her face crumpled. She sagged against the cherry newel post, her lost, expressive eyes confirming everything. "Who? How?"

Midnight knelt and picked up the football, turning it over in his hands. He spun the tire of the ten-speed and then got up. "I just know."

She started to say something, but the words couldn't get past the sudden lump in her throat.

"Don't even try," Midnight whispered, shrugging his shoulders in that arrogant way that was so like Joe's, "to defend what you've done."

"You have no right to him," she began. "Legally—"

"I have every right—the rights of a father. Do you think I give a damn about...legally? I'm a lawyer, and I know the laws a hell of a lot better than you do. And I know how to use every one of them—against you. He's my son. I've already lost the first nine years of his life because of your lies and that materialistic marriage you were so determined to make. I'm not going to lose the rest."

"He's got enough problems already."

"Is that any wonder? He senses all your unspoken lies. Every time you look at him, every time you speak to him, deep down—he knows."

"Where do you get off acting so superior? You drove me away—"

"With just cause."

"If you don't let us go we may all die, even Joe. I told you someone's after me...."

Midnight pulled out a thick clump of long white envelopes held together by a rubber band and waved them in front of her face. "I knew that long before you told me."

She gasped in horror as his brown hand ripped the rubber band in two and he yanked out several yellow clippings. "Remember these..."

Midnight shook the envelopes. Pictures of the warehouse in flames, the famous picture of Sam holding her as the warehouse burned, photographs of the Douglas house and her wedding fluttered to the tile floor.

"Every day this past month one came."

"You never said anything."

"I was playing by your rules, remember," he snarled. "Well, no more—*darling.*" The coldly uttered endearment cracked cruelly across her ragged senses as he knew it would.

"Dear God. Sam used to receive those before he was killed."

Midnight tossed the empty envelopes onto a nearby table in disgust. "That's why you're staying—with me."

"You'll be in danger, too."

"I don't give a damn about that, and neither do you."

"You're in no condition to protect us. You're too weak—"

That did it.

Some vulnerable flicker of dark emotion in his eyes filled her with remorse even before he recoiled, his face livid. He grabbed her wrist in a hard grip that hurt and yanked her against his body viciously. "I ought to show you what I could do to you—weak and impotent as you apparently think I am." His grating voice was low, but dangerous nevertheless. One brown hand was on her skin, tracing a rough line from the base of her throat, ripping the silk robe apart, and sliding lower, between her breasts, over her diaphragm and stomach to her navel, touching her in a way that made her quiver helplessly. "Don't you ever throw my weakness up to me again."

Lacy cringed away from his exploring fingers. But when they tightened painfully about her waist, she reacted to the strength of his body with another terrified shiver. He was furious, and she was afraid, and yet his insolent embrace aroused other unwanted emotions that were treacherously powerful.

She could tell by the sudden fire in his angry eyes that he felt them, too—that he hated them even more than she did.

"Let me go," she whispered.

"If only I could, but I'm as trapped in your web of lies as you are." He laughed harshly. His eyes ran over her.

She couldn't stop staring at him, either. She was so close she could see every line, every fine blue vein beneath his eyes, all the tiny scars on his brow, but these imperfections only added to his virile male appeal. She could smell him. Feel his heat. He was like a magnet. One side drew her; the other repelled her.

"Let me go," she pleaded again.

His mouth hardened. "Like I said—I'd rather spend an entire lifetime with the devil in hell than a single night with you, but there's too much at stake."

"You pigheaded, idiotic...lawyer! You always think you know everything! You always have to win! You never once listened to me!"

"For good reason."

She fought him then, hitting at him, kicking but it was no use. He was careful of his ribs this time. He'd grown up in the gutter, and even though he'd been weakened by the accident he remembered how to feint and lunge, how to avoid her blows, how to turn them to his own advantage. Soon his powerful body wrapped hers in a most humiliatingly familiar posture. Her robe had come unfastened. Her hair spilled over her shoulders. His skillful hands slid burningly against the thin silk, then inside, his touch against naked skin too knowing. He laughed harshly when she began to shiver.

"Stop fighting, unless you want more," he muttered grimly, his laughter gone. "You probably do."

His powerful arms bound her. His thighs were rock hard. So was every other part of him.

"I—I hate you," she hissed, knowing how inadequate anything she could do or say was.

He laughed in that dark, ugly way again. "But that's not all you feel."

"Take your hands off me and get out!"

She drew back her arm to slap him, but he grabbed her wrist. They were both so furiously aroused, neither of them heard the faint footstep above them on the stairs.

Curious to see the scuffle, Joe moved eagerly to the railing and tripped over his untied shoelaces and slid down two steps.

Lacy screamed as the small beloved figure tumbled toward her.

Midnight's hands fell to his sides. She raced toward her son, stopping on the bottom stair when he managed to catch the railing.

In the electric silence father and son studied each other warily. Lacy made a muted sound and covered her lips.

Moonlight shone on Joe's black hair, highlighting the silver strip above his temple. The white light washed the color from the child's dark eyes, so that they seemed opaque and otherworldly.

"Hey, mister," Joe said in his toughest, surliest voice, the voice he usually reserved for his mother. "Why were you scaring my mother?"

Midnight raised his hands as if in surrender to show he meant no harm. "Hey, you scared her worse than I did," he said gently. "You should tie your shoelaces."

Joe looked down at his shoes. "She's always telling me that, too."

Never taking his eyes off Midnight, Joe leaned down and tied his laces.

He stood up, and there was another moment of tense silence as father and son stared at one another in wary fascination.

Watching them, Lacy shivered, but the tortured name Midnight whispered sent an even icier chill through her.

"Nathan..."

Eleven

Nathan.

Moonlight sifted through the skylight, flooding the spiral stairwell and backlighting the slender boy with a ghostly radiance as Lacy lifted him into her arms to make sure he wasn't hurt.

Never able to endure displays of maternal concern, Joe squirmed free. Lacy looked so hurt, Midnight realized the gulf between mother and son might be as great as the distance between the boy and himself.

Joe tried to act tough, but his surliness had a look of loneliness that reminded Midnight of Cole at the same age. What the hell had Sam and Lacy done to Joe?

Joe hopped clumsily down another stair, ignoring the shoelace that came undone again. He scowled like Cole, but he moved like Nathan—light and quick and cocky.

"Holy cow!" Joe said, leaping down the last three stairs. He swaggered fearlessly up to the taller replica of himself. "How come you've got Halloween hair just like I do?"

"Halloween hair?"

"You know—vampire hair?"

"It runs in the family."

"Are we kin?"

"It's a long story," Midnight murmured tightly, back-pedaling fast as he knelt down and retied Joe's laces, quickly, deftly. "Too long for now."

"Are you my uncle or something?"

There was a pregnant pause. Midnight felt Lacy's eyes. And Joe's, too, growing dark and keen like he was on to them.

"Or something," Midnight said, arising.

"How come you never came around before?"

Lacy began to shiver and hugged her silk robe to her body. Although Midnight's gaze was on Joe, he was conscious of his own hostile response to her every nervous movement.

She had kept his son from him for over nine years. She had married Sam. Passed *his* son off as Sam's. Because of her, he was on tenterhooks with his own child. And he, Midnight—poor despicable fool that he was—still desired her.

"I said how come—"

Lacy, who had started down the stairs, gasped. "Joe—don't push!"

Joe's lip curled, his hostility meant solely for his mom.

"It's past your bedtime, Joe," Lacy managed in a strangled tone.

"Every time I have a serious conversation with an adult, you treat me like a baby and say something stupid, Mom."

"Because you're always up when you shouldn't be," she whispered, frantic to stop the interview.

"How can I sleep when I don't know who *he* is?"

Whitening, she chewed her lip. "His name is Johnny Midnight."

Midnight's mouth tightened. *She had told the simple truth. Not the more complex one—he's your father.*

"Why was he holding you like that? Like he was mad, but like he sorta likes you, too?"

The kid was too damned perceptive.

Joe eyed Midnight slyly. "Dad never—"

Midnight glowered.

Sam was Dad, while he was a stranger.

"Johnny's... an old friend."

Oh, was that all? Midnight's fingers coiled into fists. Her half truths were unendurable.

"Is he the guy you've been visiting in the hospital?"

"Yes," came that velvety tone that so undid Midnight.

"At least you took care of him when he was sick," Joe said in a soft, odd voice. "Why then—"

"Joe! Why do you always ask so many 'why' questions?"

"Because I want to know, Mom, and you won't tell me."

"I—I can't. Now will you please say good-night to Mr. Midnight and go to bed?"

So he was to be Mr. Midnight—to his own son. That galled him.

Joe eyed Midnight's dark face dubiously. "Will I ever see you again, Mr. Midnight?"

Midnight fought his fury toward Lacy and knelt to Joe's level. "Johnny," he ground out hoarsely. "Call me Johnny."

"I'm supposed to call grown-ups by their last names."

"I'm not just... just any grown-up. Okay?"

"Johnny." Joe eyed him in wonder. "Will I ever see you again?"

"You can bet your life on it—son."

Lacy made a queer whimpering sound.

Joe's gaze sharpened. "You ever been to Alcatraz?"

Midnight remembered the tour book in the foyer. "With your mom. A long time ago. She used to think it was a castle."

"She told me. Will you take me? My mom promised, but she always visited you instead."

"Then I owe it to you," Midnight said.

"Tomorrow?"

"Sure."

Lacy pressed her lips tightly together.

Father and son were too wrapped up in each other to notice. Then Nero came up to them and stuck his wet nose between their faces, looking from one to the other with distressed, curious eyes. Johnny and Joe laughed together.

"He gets jealous," Joe explained. "He feels left out."

Midnight's dark gaze lifted to Lacy's tense face. Moonlight gleamed in her hair and made the red silk that curved over her breasts shimmer. She personified sensuality for him, and after the long years of doing without, he felt starved for the warmth and softness of her body. Starved for her friendship, for her love as well. He wanted to take her hand and pull her down beside them.

Instead his expression hardened. "Jealous? Left out? Yeah, I can buy that. How about you, Lacy? You ever felt any of those things?" Midnight's bitter gaze fell from her to his son again too fast to see the naked spasm of uncontrollable pain slash her gentle face.

Father and son ignored her and ruffed Nero's fur.

"Joe!" Lacy said in a suffocated whisper, frantic now to separate them. "You were on your way to bed."

"No! I wasn't!"

"Yes!"

But when Lacy walked up to take Joe's hand, she tripped on a rough tile. Her leg briefly brushed Midnight's arm. He jerked his head up sharply and she jumped back, deliberately keeping her face bent low so he wouldn't see her hot cheeks.

But he saw, and his steady look made her flush deepen.

When she took hold of Joe's hand, the boy's lower lip curled and he wouldn't budge. Stubbornly he kept petting Nero, and she had to tug more desperately. Joe just hunkered lower and clung to his new friend and dog.

It was obvious to Midnight she didn't have much control over Joe, and he didn't respect her much as a result.

"Johnny—"

Midnight's eyes met hers again.

She looked so anguished, so genuinely panicked, that it was hard to regard her as the enemy.

"Please," she whispered.

There was an awful hurting silence.

She needed him.

The kid needed him.

"Please," she repeated softly, and so nicely he couldn't refuse.

"You'd better do as your mother says, or we'll both be in the doghouse along with Nero," Midnight murmured quietly, the strange paternal thrill that she had needed his help at war with his fierce antagonism toward her.

She was suffering as much as he was. He could feel it. They had a kid together, a kid who needed them both.

"Nice meeting you, Johnny," Joe said shyly, taking his hand.

Midnight's fingers closed briefly over his son's. "Nice meeting you, too. See you in the morning."

"You're sure?" Joe's lonely black eyes met his.

"I'm sure," Midnight promised softly.

Joe threw his arms around Midnight's neck. Watching this rare spontaneous gesture of affection she so craved herself from Joe, Lacy bit her lip. Only after a fierce bear hug, did he allow his mother to drag him away. At his door, Joe thought of another excuse not to go to bed.

"Mom, Mario's probably fallen asleep in front of the TV. I'd better go get him and tell him it's bedtime, too."

"No—"

"Mom—"

Lacy's eyes pleaded with Midnight again.

"I'll get Mario," Midnight said, settling the matter.

After Lacy and Joe had disappeared and Mario had gone, the silence was unbearable. Midnight went to the window. The cabbie was still parked under the streetlight.

It was ridiculous—letting her put Joe to bed when they would be leaving almost immediately. But he hadn't wanted to argue in front of Joe.

Now, Midnight wished he had. She was wasting valuable time. There was no way to know who the whispery-voiced caller was, no way to know where he was or what he was up to. The phone call could have been a setup.

Midnight was about to go get her, when she returned looking pale and fragile.

He hated the way his heart went out to her so easily. Thus, he was doubly furious when she ignored him and stalked silently to the corner of her apartment that was a kitchen, turned her back to him and squirted detergent into the sink.

"I think we hit it off," Midnight said in a low, smoldering tone from behind her.

She hit a dish so hard against the sink she probably chipped it. Running light fingertips around the edges, she said nothing.

"He liked me—and you don't like it," Midnight added, to annoy her.

"Okay! So, he liked you!" Jerkily she splashed water onto the dishes. "As if that's all that counts."

"It does to me. I always know in the first few minutes with a jury whether I'll win or lose."

She kept scrubbing that plate over and over again with furious, violent motions. "This isn't one of your damned cases."

"It's the most important case of my life, and it's beginning to feel like a win—*darling*."

"Don't call me that."

He grinned, bitterly glad the endearment had stung her as much as it had him.

The wet plate slipped through her fingertips and shattered. Her cheeks white, her violet eyes enormous, she whirled around. Her hands dripped water onto the floor as she flung down the rag. "How could you lead him on like that? He's usually so quiet. You had him asking me all kinds of questions."

"Maybe you should have answered them."

"You bast—"

"Hey, hey... Wait a minute now. Don't get me started asking how could *you* do everything *you* did. You kept my child. You passed him off as Sam's. How the hell do you think that feels?"

"Well, now you know about Joe. You've seen him and made a hit with him. So, will you go?"

"Great idea! Get your bags. His, too."

"Johnny—"

"I'm as tired of these games as you are. You're both moving in with me."

"You hate me."

Midnight's black brows drew together and his eyes narrowed, even as his cynical mouth lifted in an ironic smile. "Do you really think so, Slim, my precious...darling?" He moved nearer, near enough to inhale the rose scent that perfumed her slender throat, near enough to murmur, near enough to feel the heat of her, near enough to speak softly in her ear. "I think hate is an easy, colorless word that doesn't begin to describe the difficult, complex, negative feelings I have for you."

He stooped and picked up a jagged sliver of white china. "Careful, Slim, you might hurt yourself."

"How can you be so monstrously selfish?"

Midnight arched his brow innocently and flicked the broken bit toward the wastebasket, proud when he made it. "Me? If ever the pot berated the kettle, Slim—"

"Think of what this will do to Joe."

"That's all I am thinking of—my son, Joe." The sentence was a deliberate insult. "He needs me. Do you know who he reminds me of, almost more than Nathan? He reminds me of Cole, at the same age."

"No. How can you say that?"

"Because it's the truth. He's been neglected. He walks all over you, but deep down he's hungry for your love and attention." *The same as I am.*

"Which I will give him, if you let us go."

"Raising a child is hard for a woman alone. Without a father, in a few more years he'll be completely out-of-control."

"What about us? How can we live together under the same roof like some reconciled couple?"

"The last thing I want is a reconciliation. You'll have your precious privacy, your own room, your own bed. I'd rather sleep with the devil than you."

"I'd prefer a cobra."

"There! We're more compatible than you think."

"You have an odd definition of compatibility."

Midnight couldn't resist reaching out and taking her face between his lean, hard hands. The instant his rough fingers touched satin-warm skin, he knew he'd made a mistake. As he slid his fingers through her silver hair, she froze, too, her strangled breath catching in her throat.

"You have even odder definitions of truth and loyalty and trust, Slim. I loved you. And you chose Sam."

When he withdrew his hands, she backed away, swallowing convulsively. He felt equally shaken.

He grabbed her suitcase to distract himself.

When it wouldn't latch, he yanked it apart and began to stuff flimsy silken garments inside—slips, lacy panties, bras, blouses, negligees. The cool stuff rasped against his callused fingertips. Which was all it took to keep him turned on.

She was right—he was mad to think they could live together. But he had no choice. Flushing hotly, he slammed the lid, snapping the latches even though silk still dripped out of the cracks. The bag had rollers so he gave it a push that sent it sliding across the uneven tiles, rattling loudly and crashing into the door.

"Are you going to pack Joe's stuff or will I?" he thundered.

"We're not going anywhere with you."

His mouth hardened into a grim line. "That argument is over, sweetheart. You're going if I have to drag you screaming out of this apartment, and Joe, too. You can either pack his clothes or leave them. But I'm not leaving you here so that bastard can kill you at his leisure."

"I can take care of myself—"

"Maybe. But I can do it better."

"Because you're a man?"

"Because I'll do whatever it takes to stop him—"

"Johnny, no—"

Her pleading was cut off by a branch snapping outside in the wind and Nero's vicious snarl. Joe's door banged as the Doberman leapt out of it and raced to the front door.

Joe came out of his bedroom, wild-eyed, dragging a heavy bat. "Someone's out there," he whispered fiercely.

Johnny caught his ankle and pulled him to the floor. "Get down." He grabbed Lacy's hand, yanking her to the floor, too.

Midnight left them huddled together while he crawled about the apartment turning off lights.

Then he opened the front door and an icy gust swept inside. The alarm went off, and Nero raced outside and down the famous Filbert Steps, plunging clumsily through the thorny bushes of the darkened rose garden.

A shriek came from behind the rose-covered lattices at the far wall. A dark hooded figure thrashed noisily up a trellis with Nero lunging and nipping at its heels. Then the figure levered its slim body over the high wall, and Nero bayed helplessly.

Midnight would have followed if Lacy hadn't seized him. With a strength born of terror she clung to his arm. The cold wind blew her silken hair back from her chalky face. "Don't go, Johnny."

Midnight hesitated, a muscle jerking in his taut jaw. Was her concern real, or was it another lie?

Her anxious fingers pressed into his. "Sam was murdered while I listened," she whispered.

Sam. Always Sam. Whatever tenderness her desperate fear might have aroused dissolved with that despised name.

Hateful jealousy filling him, Midnight disentangled her icy fingers and regarded her with scathing indifference. "Cheer up. Maybe you'll get lucky and I'll die, too."

Lacy caught his white cotton sleeve, sobbing. "I love you."

His black gaze riveted to hers. "Right! You slept with me, but you married Sam and passed off my son as his. You were taking him away tomorrow."

"I loved you—even after that last afternoon. Even on my wedding day. And because I did, Sam and I never had a real marriage."

Just her saying that made Midnight want to hold her and kiss her, to forget everything she'd ever done, to forget every lie she'd ever told, to forget even that she'd been running away tonight—taking Joe with her.

But Midnight's cold, cynical mind wouldn't allow him to soften. His furious eyes blazed daggers. "You've always been a liar. And you were never better than now."

"I love you." She held on to him, her whole body heaving in silent anguish.

She was soft and velvet warm. He should break her neck for what she was doing to him, but for the life of him he couldn't push her away. And her sweet pretenses tore more hunks out of his heart than her cruelest cuts.

Lightning sizzled, and a savage, cold wind rushed up the hill and banged the door behind him against the wall. Raindrops began to pelt the earth as violently as bullets. Lacy was wearing only her thin silk robe. Despite Midnight's heated nearness, she began to shiver.

Then Nero howled insanely, and Midnight came to his senses and shrugged free, shielding her from the cold with his tall body.

She shrank against the wall, her face stricken and white. "Johnny, you're hurt. Don't go—"

"Save the lies. For now take care of our son. Nothing else between you and me will ever matter again."

Then Midnight hurled himself out into the chill, wet night.

But the last thing he heard was the soft, terrified sound of his name as she called after him.

The cabbie's dim reading light was a blurry beacon in the downpour.

The hooded intruder in the ski mask, raced toward it, but the Doberman was catching up fast.

A hundred yards.

To safety.

Tongue lolling, vicious claws scraping wet asphalt and scrambling through muddy potholes, the ugly dog was closing the gap.

With a bursting chest, the figure in black fell against the cab just as Johnny Midnight leapt out onto the street.

Panicky black-gloved fingers grappled with the slick rear-door handle, and then the intruder was collapsing inside, snapping automatic door locks, gasping, laughing hysterically, gleefully yanking something black and shiny and heavy out of a rain-soaked pocket.

Too late.

Nero threw himself against the window, slobbering messily, and howling wildly. Then Midnight was there instead of the dog, and the killer pointed the .38 dead center between his two black eyebrows.

Nighty night.

The trigger was squeezed—hard.

There was an awful, disappointing click.

And nothing happened.

The startled cabbie turned around, bewildered by the pandemonium and then terrified when the snub-nosed bluish barrel jerked toward him.

"Drive or die," compelled a furious choked whisper from behind the black ski mask.

The cabbie jammed his foot down hard on the accelerator. A long time later he asked, "Where to?"

"Sausalito. The marina."

Twelve

Lacy sprang up in bed, her heart beating wildly, not knowing which of the strange sounds had awakened her in the chill, howling darkness—*because there were so many.* She'd always hated boats with their dank smells of salt and sea, but never more than this stormy night when she and Joe were Johnny's prisoners.

Wind clawed at the shingles and rain drummed against her window. Even in Sausalito's protected harbor, the swells slashed the hull, gently rocking Johnny's houseboat, so that it seemed a shadowy living thing.

The bow and stern groaned uneasily against the straining lines. Other creaking sounds made her heart race and her stomach lurch as she imagined furtive footsteps on the deck outside. When she leaned toward her window, the sky exploded, turning the inside of her bedroom phosphorescent blue and then black again. Thunder rolled.

Surely no one could be out there.

Pulling her thin silk robe over her white ruffled night-gown, she got up for the third time, and stumbled out into the hall to check on Joe. Midnight's door was still ajar, and she was drawn to his threshold.

He had forced her here—against her will.

She shouldn't have the slightest interest in him.

But she did.

He had thrown off his covers and his black head was slumped awkwardly upon his white pillow, his long body boneless. He'd tossed his shoes to the floor, but he'd fallen asleep in his clothes with his light on. She remembered how gray faced he'd been when they'd first arrived. Even so he had grimly ransacked his drawers for his gun and bullets, while she'd angrily struggled to put Joe to bed.

Joe had been too aware of the tensions between them and too excited by the novelty of Johnny's houseboat in Sausa-lito to sleep. In the end, she'd had to beg Johnny to help her. Which he had done with a lazy, superior grin and madden-ing ease. Joe had crawled into his bed and shut his eyes as docilely as a lamb while Midnight sat beside him, oiling his hateful gun. Johnny, who had always had such a way with other people's children, was equally gifted with his own.

She didn't want to think about that.

Even in sleep Midnight looked so terrifyingly weary that she felt compelled to hover. His shirt was crisp and snowy white—stretched taut across his dark skin, but he had un-buttoned several buttons, and the air was so cold she was shivering. He was thin from his long convalescence. Too thin. And weaker—although he was too proud to admit it.

She saw the woolly scarlet blanket clumped at the foot of his bed and suddenly, even though she wished she didn't care, she worried that he might catch a chill and have some sort of relapse. Surely she could slip inside and pull his blanket over him without him knowing.

She tiptoed toward him, gathering up the red blanket, carefully stepping across his shoes, leaning over him and gently smoothing the woolly quilt over his broad shoulders.

She hardly dared to breathe as she tucked the covers about him. Yet she wanted to linger, to press the red wool close against his warm tanned cheek, to touch him, to stroke his black hair, even to lie down beside him and find comfort in his strength—in spite of everything that was wrong between them.

Instead she pulled the chain of the lamp, and the room melted into velvet darkness made magic by the glistening wet night and the roar of the sea. By his presence in the bed.

He stirred. For a long, hushed moment she froze in the silvery moonlight and studied the sparkling raindrops trailing like a shower of diamonds down his windows. The sweet smell of rain made her remember that tender night when she'd given him her body and pledged her love to him forever.

Suddenly she was too aware of the indolent stretch of his long, muscular body. Too aware of an unwanted trill of feminine sensation. Too aware of the long years of loneliness.

Thunder reverberated through the air. Tight throated, she gasped at the keening violence of the wind. At the keening violence inside herself.

She had to get out of his room.

She was stealthily sneaking toward the cracked door when she tripped over one of his shoes and gave a startled little cry.

Suddenly a huge shadow blocked the silvery light from the window. A fierce hand swooped down from behind her, clamping over her mouth, smothering the rest of her incoherent scream. A cold metal barrel pushed against her throat as she was half dragged, half carried across the carpet and shoved against the wall. Her assailant stood her up and stretched her hands high above her head, pushing her arms widely apart, spreading her legs, too, and bracing them against the cold wooden wall, pinioning her so that her breasts were mashed flat by his immense, hot male body.

The gun dug deeper into her throat.

Her terrified heart began pounding like a jackhammer. But no faster than his.

"When I let you go, leave your hands where they are," he ordered coldly, "while I search you."

"Johnny—"

He jerked back appalled.

"Who else?" She whirled, equally outraged, her eyes flying to his dark, stunned face and then to the .357 Magnum that he slowly lowered and placed with a thunk on the table beside his bed.

Awkwardly he fumbled for the chain and snapped on the light. When he lifted his harsh chiseled face again, he looked so cruel and angry her own scowl deepened. Which made his obsidian black eyes darken with even greater displeasure.

She attacked first. "I—I told you, you'd shoot the wrong person with that thing." She rubbed her bruised throat and looked past him to his gun. "You force me to move in with you—to protect me. Then you—"

His dark face flushed guiltily. "What the hell were you doing in here anyway?" he demanded furiously.

The scarlet blanket had fallen to the floor. Stalling, she leaned down, picked it up and folded it slowly, never thinking as he watched her how that might seem a wifely gesture, how that might set his thoughts along the wrong path. "I got up to check on Joe."

"So—what the hell were you doing in here?"

"I—I . . ." Guilt stricken, she dropped the blanket at the foot of his bed.

"Don't lie."

"You always think the worst of me."

"I wonder why?"

Scarlet wool blurred as she thought of how tenderly she had tucked the blanket around him. He wouldn't want to know that, and she didn't want to tell him. So she couldn't look at him lest he suspect.

She straightened stiffly, and felt his hard eyes boring into her slim back when she turned to go.

"I'm sorry," he said suddenly in a hoarse strangled tone that sounded so vulnerable she was caught off guard.

"What?" Her own voice was suddenly stilted and unnatural.

"For scaring you," he whispered. "For the gun. It was under my pillow."

He had stooped to pick up the blanket. Slowly, thoughtfully he stared at it. Puzzled, he looked up at her.

She turned. And then he knew.

In the golden light he was darkly, dangerously handsome. A tremor went through her, then a whirlpool of dizzying feelings. "I—I heard a sound," she said weakly. "That's all. I wanted to check on Joe."

"For the third time?" he demanded, his voice huskier.

So, he had not been sleeping all that deeply.

She looked away.

"That was a risky thing to do—coming in here."

"I know."

"I might have hurt you." His tone was strangely gentle.

As always the barriers were there—his deep distrust of her, his fury, her own hurt and the fact that he'd forced her to move in with him despite the danger. And all the other pain-filled unmet needs that tormented them. But the unexpected kindness in his eyes and the concern in his low voice made her ache for all that they had lost, for the impossibility of some half-fathomed shared future of radiant happiness they'd once dreamed of, which now would always be forbidden.

He took a single step toward her. She backed away, into a pool of golden lamplight that revealed the purpling mark on her neck his gun and rough hands had made.

He sucked in his breath. Two swift steps propelled his tall,
lithe body to hers.

She felt the strong grip of his hands on her arms, pulling
her to him, and she looked up into his grave black eyes. Instinctively she pulled away when his hand reached toward
her face. But his searching fingers brushed the tender bruise
at her throat caressingly. She cried out softly and jumped
away, feeling terribly self-conscious beneath his gaze.

"See, I did hurt you. You'll be black-and-blue tomorrow. You already are." He looked sickened and shamed, his
troubled countenance filled with self-loathing. "I don't
blame you for being afraid of me when I forced you here
and then—"

She shook her head wildly. "No—" His gentleness made
her more uncomfortable than his violence. "That's not why
I'm afraid of you."

"Then why?" he demanded.

Unhappily she tore her gaze from his face.

*Because I can't be near you without remembering how it
was with us, without wanting you, without craving your
touch, your kindness, your love—all your precious gifts I so
carelessly threw away. Because I can't admit I came in here
tonight because I still love you.*

She started to turn.

He cut her off at the door. His dark face was taut with
intense emotion. "Lacy—"

Her pride would not let her speak, and neither would his.
But as she looked at him there was a profound gentleness in
his smile, and a heated wanting in his eyes.

He removed her robe and pulled her to him with unsteady hands that burned her skin. As those large hands slid
over her they lit little fires, and a small animal sound escaped her parted lips.

She didn't know how adorably young she looked in her
white ruffled nightgown—how much she seemed the sweet
girl he'd once loved completely, irrevocably. Or how little

she seemed the society hostess whom he'd believed had scorned him.

Caught in a fiery golden dream, she closed her eyes. He wrapped his arms around her slim waist and pressed her into his body, holding her closely, stroking her shining silver hair and lower back in a slow, rhythmic way that was deeply comforting. She had never felt such lulling warmth as that of his body next to hers.

"Lacy," he began hoarsely. He brought his mouth to her injured throat and kissed her, nuzzling her velvet flesh, inhaling her sweet woman smell. He kissed her closed eyelids, her lashes, and every kiss made tiny flames leap just beneath the surface of her skin.

"Lacy—" He was almost humble as he tipped back her chin and studied her lovely flushed features and then smiled in a self-deprecating manner. "There's so much I have to say."

There was so much she had to make up for.

But she was never to know what might have happened next, because Joe screamed and the fragile spell of that tantalizing moment of shared closeness was shattered.

His arms tightened and then fell away. When his face hardened subtly, a bitter shell closed over the fragile new tenderness in her own heart. The soft light dying in her eyes, she, too, locked the precious moment away.

"Mommy!"

Lacy pushed past him in swift, light steps, and Midnight raced after her.

Joe's eyes were wide and glittering even though Nero was lounging protectively beside him.

For once Joe didn't resist his mother when she cradled him in her arms. "What's the matter, darling?"

Joe's dark head snuggled against her ruffled bosom. "I heard something outside! And my light wouldn't turn on." Joe blinked fiercely, fighting his tears.

Johnny snapped at the chain on the lamp several times. "What the hell? I could swear the thing was working—" He caught himself. "The bulb's out. I'll get another one."

Joe's huge excited gaze went to the gun now tucked inside Midnight's belt. "Why do you have your .357 Magnum?"

Lacy frowned. "And how do you even know what it is, young man?"

"Dad had a catalogue. Besides Johnny told me about it when he cleaned it."

Raising her eyes back to Johnny, she saw his bronzed face tighten at the mention of Sam. "Johnny, I told you I didn't want you to frighten Joe with that gun."

"Unlike you, I think it's necessary to face hard truths," Midnight said shortly. "He's not scared of the gun—you are. He needs to know about it. Even if I hadn't showed it to him, kids always know everything. They're natural snoops. They sift through everything. I bet Sam's catalogue wasn't sitting on the coffee table."

"It was on the top shelf of his closet inside a box!" Joe said.

Midnight's eyes bored into hers.

"I want you to get rid of the gun, Johnny."

"Don't be dumb, Mom. I bet the other guy has one."

"Which is why we should never have come here."

Johnny stared at her for a long time. "Which is why I have to take care of you," he said at last.

"How can I fight you both?" she whispered.

Their identical smiles were very male and very superior.

"Get a light bulb, Mom!"

"They're in the kitchen. In the cabinet to the right of the stove," Midnight murmured conspiratorially.

On her way back from the kitchen with the new bulb she heard Joe's piping voice from the hall.

"I wish I had a gun like you do. Then I'd feel safe."

Lacy stepped inside his room and felt betrayed again when she saw Midnight's great body hunkered low beside Joe as he showed off his gun to the enraptured child. Johnny was even encouraging him to reverently touch the black handle.

Lacy glared at Midnight accusingly. "I thought I told you—"

"Hey, why don't you let me handle this one, Slim?"

"Because—" She looked into his dark face and was stopped by the depth of what she saw that he already felt for his son.

"You know I hate guns, weapons of any sort."

"If they're around, ignorance is more dangerous than knowledge. Trust me," Midnight said quietly.

Let me teach him what he needs to know, his eyes said.

Such a simple request. But it filled her with terror and with guilt for the nine years he'd lost with Joe.

Johnny was a father—a man. There were things he could teach Joe that would always be beyond her.

She got up and walked toward the door.

"Do you think I'm a coward?" she heard Joe ask in a small, confiding voice when she leaned against the wall outside in the hall.

Joe almost never talked to her.

"Just 'cause you're afraid?" Midnight asked casually, and then shook his head. "No."

"I've always been scared of the dark."

"So was I—when I was a kid. I had an older brother, Nathan, who wasn't scared of anything. But he used to tease me to make me even more scared—not that I ever let on. But he knew, 'cause brothers always know. He made up stories about a terrible prehistoric monster called a raptaroo that was sort of a giant bat that could see and smell little kids it wanted to eat in the dark. He said raptaroos were always flying into little boy's windows and gobbling them."

What a story to tell a scared little boy.

"For real?" Joe asked, avid for more.

"No, Nathan just had a vivid imagination. There's no such thing as a raptaroo."

"Good."

The rain glistened against the windows and pounded on the roof. Lacy knew she was eavesdropping, but Johnny had never told her this story before and like Joe she wanted to hear the rest of it.

"Well, one night someone broke into our house. Nathan got out his baseball bat same as you did tonight, but I . . . I was a coward and I locked myself in my closet. Nathan called to me in the middle of that terrible fight, but I just covered my ears. The guy was twice as big as Nathan, but it was so dark, and Nathan knew the apartment and he clobbered him with the bat."

"A bat like mine?"

"Yes. After that Nathan was the big hero on our block, and I was the coward. Nathan used to fight the bullies off me—till he got killed. Then I had to fight my own battles. But I was always scared, more scared than ever after Nathan died. Our family was never the same again."

"How'd he die?"

"He got run over on his bike. Hit-and-run. They never caught the guy."

"Are you still scared?"

"Not since the car accident."

"Will you stay with me—till I fall asleep?"

"Shut your eyes . . . and don't think about raptaroos."

"How'd you know my brain was popping about 'em?"

"I just knew," came that deep, gentle baritone.

"What color are they?"

"Red and purple. But don't think about them."

"Do they have beaks?"

"Long teeth, too."

"Feathers?"

"Just a few. Mostly scales."

"Are they slimy?"

"You're supposed to be going to sleep."

"You're my real dad, aren't you?"

Out of the blue, without warning, Joe's question knocked the breath out of her.

Lacy swallowed hard, and her heartbeat seemed to rush in her ears as she waited for Midnight's answer.

There was a long silence. The raindrops raced like diamonds down the windows.

"Yes," came Johnny's voice, gentler than she'd ever heard it.

She felt so tense she could barely breathe.

"How come you never came before?"

"Because I didn't know."

"Will you stay with us always?" Joe asked very softly.

Hysterical laughter bubbled up inside her. Joe didn't know that what he longed for, what she longed for, too, was impossible.

Not waiting to hear how Midnight would reply, she stumbled toward the glistening window at the end of the hall.

But his husky whisper followed her there.

"You'll have to ask your mother."

Putting her trembling fingers against the icy glass, she traced the path of a brilliant droplet.

And then another.

Then her eyes filled with tears at the impossibility of her half-formed dreams and Joe's. The raindrops blurred. She splayed her fingers on the slick transparent surface helplessly, hopelessly and began to shake with silent anguish.

A long time later she heard a hushed footfall on the carpet. An indrawn breath when Midnight saw her there. She didn't dare turn around.

"Where are the raindrops going so fast?" his deep voice asked huskily from the darkness behind her.

Thirteen

"**W**here are the raindrops going so fast?" The second time he said it, Midnight's voice grated so bitterly, it froze her heart. "That was a sappy line if I ever heard one. Forgive me—I was only a poor fool of twenty-one. And I loved you. At least I thought I did. But the sweet, innocent girl I loved never existed."

"You weren't exactly my tender heroic prince either, Johnny Midnight. You turned on me the first chance you got."

His mouth twisted as he stalked toward her. "I had a hell of a good reason. Hey, but maybe I was lucky to find disillusionment so young. The rest of my life—even the accident—has been easy after you. Easy until I learned you were the mother of my child, and you'd made my own son a stranger to me."

"I called you once after I married, but you were so cold. And I was so terrified. What was the point of telling you when you despised me?"

"How the hell can you ask that?"

Lacy whirled away from Midnight, not wanting to reveal more of the deep emotions she felt for him. But he caught her in that shimmering darkness, his dark face ravaged and wild. Then he roughly kissed away the tears that sparkled as brightly as raindrops upon her pale cheeks.

"Oh, God," he groaned even as he pressed her into his body and his hand came up to caress the delicate lines of her face. "Why do your tears twist me in knots when I should be crying, not you? You kept Joe from me. For nine damned years. You taught him Sam was his father. You tricked me into accepting a scholarship to Stanford Law School that was really blood money from Sam. I should hate you. Maybe I do. But, God, I still want you, too."

Midnight buried his face in the wealth of her flowing hair. Then his hot seeking lips brushed across her nape, leaving her skin feeling overheated and raw. His angry mouth moved to her throat.

"Lacy," he moaned, his tone low and tortured and furious as he drank in the taste of her. "Do you know what you do to me?"

She felt his burning rage, but she felt his feverish desire, too.

"God, you tear me apart."

"I—I don't want this...." she managed in a hushed whisper, struggling to push him away.

His arms closed around her, pulling her to him so she fitted him snugly, so that she could have no doubts about the state of his arousal. "Neither do I," he growled.

"Not like this," she begged, "when you almost hate me."

"After what you've done, how else could it ever be for us?"

"You were so cold. And you called me a tramp like my mother. For years every time I thought of you I remembered how hard your face was when you said it, how filled with hate your eyes were. How like my father—"

Midnight's blistering mouth moved over Lacy's with urgency. His tongue thrust undeterred, deep into her mouth, and his lips clung to hers in a shattering kiss. With his mouth fused to hers, he picked her up and carried her to his bedroom. "Once I didn't care what you were because I wanted you more than anything. But you wanted everything money could buy more than you ever wanted me."

"No—"

He set her down. His hands slid her robe from her shoulders and it pooled at her feet. His eyes were dark and unfathomable. "You didn't live with the Douglases six months before you began to think you were too good for me. The night my father died you let Sam throw me out his back door like I was garbage. His thugs held me down. One of them put a boot to my throat and kicked me down the stairs. I stayed out there an hour, bleeding, groveling like a dog, hoping you might come to me."

She turned away, ashamed. "I—I didn't know. I was young, confused. So much had happened to us. You were so locked up in your own pain. So dark and furious most of the time. Your grades fell, and you had to drop out of law school. You got that job as a longshoreman and started running around with that rough bunch. You drank every night. You would stay away from me for days. Then when I saw you, you were always angry. I wasn't sure you loved me any more. And that night, when Sam had you thrown out, I was too angry at you and too caught up in the excitement of the Douglas Christmas party. I was so eager to show the Douglases I could be an elegant hostess, and you came and were so rude and determined to spoil everything."

Midnight stiffened. "My father died that night."

"But you didn't tell me till later."

"Because I was furious that you seemed to care more for them than for me. Every day you seemed more impressed by Sam and money."

"I'm sorry for that night. But not for learning social graces or trying to teach them to you."

"You did a hell of a lot more than that. You remade yourself from the inside out. You spent all your time with those snobs. Then you married Sam."

"But you were terrible to me, Johnny. Do you remember our last afternoon together. You'd just finished law school—"

He nodded bitterly. Those final hours were burned like a shameful brand across his soul. By then all he'd wanted was revenge, and he'd found a sordid use for her sweetness.

"Oh, Johnny, that last day when you made love to me, I got pregnant with Joe. How can you blame me for not telling you about him when you called me a tramp and threw me out?"

"I felt a thousand times worse than you that day," Midnight said quietly.

"It was the first time you'd called me since that night your father died. I came to you eagerly because I'd been hoping so long you'd call. I loved you."

"You came to me to get what you got—sex," he whispered through gritted teeth. "Even though you planned to marry Sam."

"I was going to marry him because I was lonely, because I'd lost you. Because I was young and impressionable and I'd read about him in books and newspapers, and I thought he was something he wasn't. He'd been kind to me. No one but you had ever been kind, and you'd grown hard and cold. You wouldn't even look at me if we happened to run into each other on campus. I thought you were finished with me forever."

"When I found out you'd sold me out to Sam I had to get even."

"I only did what I did to help you. You were working so hard just to survive. The scholarship was funded anonymously, so you'd never know. I never understood why Sam told you.''

"Because he wanted me to know that he'd bought me the same as he'd bought you.''

"I just wanted to give you a chance to be what I knew you could be.''

"A lawyer. A money-machine. In case your little romance with Sam didn't pan out. Was that why you were so friendly when I finally graduated and called you? Were you still hedging your bets?''

"No, Johnny." She trembled violently. She wanted to go to him, but his fierce black eyes held her at bay.

She went on. "I—I told Sam after you made love to me that last time I couldn't marry him, that I loved you and could never be a true wife to him, that I was pregnant and would have to go away. He used the baby to convince me to marry him, saying the baby needed a father. We never had a real marriage. He never liked Joe because Joe reminded him of you.''

"For a woman like you, I'm sure money was enough.''

"Oh, Johnny." She studied him wordlessly for a long moment and then turned away and walked to the glistening window, so he wouldn't see her cry. But her muted voice was choked. "You can be so stupid and so blind sometimes.''

She touched the icy glass, and its coldness seeped inside her. The last afternoon came back to her with shattering force. She had lain in his arms still shuddering from his violent lovemaking as he'd eased his lean body from hers and whispered the savage words that had torn her to pieces.

"Your father warned me what you were—a hot-blooded tramp on the make—like your mother—who'd sell herself to the highest bidder no matter who or what he was. But your passion will betray you because you'll want what only I can give you, and you'll die a little every day you're married to Sam Douglas instead of me.''

He had traced his hands over her body one last time until he had her shivering and dying for him again. Then he had taken her brutally, and she had gloried even in that soul-destroying mating. He'd gotten up, just as shaken as she and dressed silently and furiously while she'd watched him with tormented eyes. He'd come back to the bed and kissed her, almost sweetly, and then with the coldest voice he'd ever used, he'd said, "Let me be the first to congratulate you on the brilliant marriage you're about to make—darling."

"I'll never marry him now," she had whispered.

"Oh, but you will."

And she had because of Joe.

The rain lashed the houseboat. Lacy buried her face in her hands, wishing she could stop crying, but she couldn't. She had relived that awful last afternoon thousands of times, and it had never lost its power.

But just as she'd relived Midnight's coldness and her own heartbroken misery, she had relived the swirling madness of their bittersweet passion as well. He had shown her that even his hatred could be sweet stormy darkness where the only feeling was his lips on her body, moving burningly over flushed skin like liquid fire, the only sensation, those hot waves of wild need coursing through her.

Even when he'd sworn he despised her, he'd made love to her with soul-destroying passion. She's surrendered herself to him in love, and she loved him still.

He had played on all her emotions when he'd taken his revenge that day—even the one that was the deepest and the most all-abiding—her eternal love for him.

Maybe it was time she took her own revenge.

She ran the back of her hands across her tear-wet face and drew in a deep, calming breath. Then she squared her shoulders and faced him.

"You of all men should know a woman like me would want more from a man than money," she breathed huskily, gliding toward him in the semidarkness with a determined look that caused him to back away from her till he hit the wall. "Well, I'm tired of money, and you're the only man I've ever wanted. You've haunted me, Johnny Midnight. I've hated you and I've loved you. But most of all I've wanted you."

Something in her voice made his eyes go hot as they trailed over her, making her feel even more like a wanton.

She touched him with silky, sliding fingertips that moved down the length of him, flowing, squeezing, and the instant her hand closed over him, he convulsed at the wave of pulsing desire that coursed through him.

She giggled softly at her power, brought her hands around his neck and her lips next to his.

"Lacy, what the hell are you doing?"

"You know exactly what I'm doing."

"Lacy—"

"Hush. Why did you bring me into your bedroom if you didn't intend to make love to me?"

"I don't know."

"Then I'll have to show you, the way you showed me that last afternoon. Maybe you're not the only one who ever needed revenge in the bedroom."

"No—"

"Oh, yes! Johnny, yes—" She moaned softly and unbuttoned her nightgown and let it slide slowly downward, revealing the voluptuous curves of her naked body in the silvery light. She looked at him with large wet eyes. A faint smile curved her lips. "I know that after head injuries, some patients feel ill at ease the first time. Maybe a little afraid that they can't perform—"

"It isn't that," he ground out, furious, completely seduced by the need to prove himself.

"I didn't think so," she whispered, her violet eyes glowing triumphantly that he'd fallen so easily for her ploy.

She came into his arms, but he was rigidly still at first. She trailed scorching fingertips across his shoulders, his neck and along his ears and moved against him. "There hasn't been anyone—ever—except you," she whispered. "I married Sam, but I never slept with him. No matter what I did, no matter how I hurt you, you and you alone, have been my only love."

You and you alone have been my only love.
Midnight studied her beautiful upturned face and read the shining light in her eyes.
Her only love.
A lump of nameless emotion constricted his throat.
Oh, my God. He despised himself for almost believing her.

Did she think him such a weakened brain-damaged sap he would fall for a line like that? He forced himself to remember she'd been planning to take Joe away from him forever.

"Damn you! Don't say anything else," he muttered thickly, his rasping tone rent with pain.

She swallowed a sob, as his jaw set in a ruthless line.

"Johnny, love me," she whispered.

The velvet sound quivered through every male nerve in his body, snapping what was left of his fragile control.

She saw the wild look on his face, and didn't resist when he pulled her to him.

His hands moved over her.

Her body was different, better. Her breasts were fuller. Her hunger greater.

So was his.

Heated needs pulsed through him as he carried her to the bed and ripped the covers back. Then he tore off his clothes and lay down on the cool tangle of sheets beside her.

He took no time for tenderness.

He fused his hard mouth with hers, rolled on top of her and pushed inside her. She cried out at the pain, and even though his heated body felt tense and strained to plunge more deeply, he went as still as death.

He didn't move, but the voluptuous warmth of her tight body penetrated his whole being. He had hurt her. *She had told him she'd never let Sam touch her.* She had told the truth, at least, in part—she hadn't made love for a long, long time.

A wave of tenderness washed over him, and Midnight began to kiss her more gently than he'd ever kissed her. His hands caressed her soft skin with a reverence that so touched her soul she began to weep soundlessly.

He wanted to cherish her, to protect her, to love her—he made her know that with his lips, his hands and his powerful body.

Then the heat of his desire for her mingled with those gentler feelings, and his passion intensified. He began to breathe hard and fast. When he thrust deeply into her, she welcomed him, trembling, clinging, her nails digging into his back before she seemed to realize she might be hurting him. He smothered her satiny mouth, her ears, her throat with violent kisses, as though he could never get enough of her.

Within seconds their passion grew so fevered that they both dissolved in mutual volcano-hot climaxes.

Afterward he drew her into his arms, his perspiring body collapsing in the velvet warmth of her tender embrace. He'd gone too fast, but it was the highest physical gratification he had ever known.

When she tried to get up, his hard hand closed around her waist and pulled her snugly back, holding her, saying nothing, promising nothing.

But the hateful throbbing need he felt for her hadn't been assuaged by that one time. Then he cynically remembered once had never been enough for her, either, and he touched her intimately, stroking her inside with his fingers, thrilling when she shivered and cried out for him to take her.

He went slower, and she felt better to him because he took time to savor her. Again he made no promises, no vows, but his body's passion did it for him. Even if his stubborn will refused to be bound to her, she was part of the secret silent rhythm of his heated flesh.

But if she suspected that his lips flamed so hotly only against hers, that his body ached with such savage, unwanted needs solely for her, that his emotions went deeper than lust, he was determined not to let her be sure.

She had said she wanted revenge. Well, so did he. The last thing he wanted to betray to her was that his need of her—more than even his injuries—made him know he was despicably weak. If she had wanted to flex her sensual power over him, he was equally determined to keep her in the dark about the extent of that power. She had his love. She owned every part of him. But he was not about to tell her.

So afterward when he was satiated and felt languorous in the golden aftermath of their lovemaking, when he might have buried his face in her throat and kissed her tenderly, he rolled away as coldly as he had that terrible long-ago afternoon.

Lacy lay shivering in the chilly darkness. Midnight lay sprawled tensely beside her, his arms crossed under his head. It crushed her that now his hunger was spent, he no longer seemed to feel the need for any closeness with her.

After such incredible warmth, how could he treat her with such callous indifference?

Johnny had given her passion. He had even been tender. But the moment it was over he acted like she was of no further importance to him.

He didn't move when she reached down and pulled the covers to her throat, but she knew his eyes were open. His face was set and grim. He was staring up into the darkness, too.

She remembered how glorious their lovemaking had once been, when they'd been young and felt naively sure of each other. What she missed so keenly was that wonderful feeling of soul-to-soul bonding.

His icy voice sent more chills through her. "Happy, Lacy?"

"What do you mean?" she whispered, terrified.

"You wanted revenge in the bedroom, and you damn sure got it. You showed us both that the real thing isn't nearly as good as our fantasies."

"Because we loved each other then," she cried in a tight throbbing voice, wishing he wouldn't be so cruel, wishing he'd just take her in his arms again.

But he didn't, so she got up.

The sheets fell away. For a moment his savage gaze flickered over her naked body. His eyes lit with a hot light. Then he rolled on his other side, as if he couldn't bear the sight of her.

Hurriedly she pulled on her nightgown.

As she opened the door, she heard him get up and yank on his jeans. She waited for a heartbeat outside his room, half hoping he'd follow her.

Instead she heard his bed creak as he threw himself back down with a sigh of disgust. Another long moment passed. His mattress groaned as he thrashed angrily first onto one side and then the other.

He wasn't coming.

More than anything, she wanted to crawl back to him and beg him to love her.

She ran down the hall to her own room instead. When she pushed open the door, her room was icy cold—even colder than Johnny's. The window was open and her bed was drenched. The wind surged and a frigid blast of rain hit her.

Behind her the door clicked shut. A dark figure was standing in the shadows blocking the only exit.

"Johnny—"

But the man at the door was too young to be Johnny. He had red hair not black and his eyes were electric blue.

She tried to scream, but her vocal cords wouldn't work.

"Don't be afraid, Lacy, it's only me," came his awful choked whisper.

Cole Douglas stepped toward her. His face was thin and parchment white, but his wild eyes blazed fiercely. He shuffled toward her, his slow gait that of a zombie, and she could only stand there in frozen terror. Unable to speak, unable to move, she felt trapped in a living nightmare.

Only when his thin wet hand reached for her, did she scream. He grabbed her and she kicked wildly. A gust of wind made the houseboat rock, and he pitched forward, seizing her, his wiry body dragging her down beneath him. His quick breaths fell raggedly against her neck. His cold hands fell against her throat.

He was going to choke her.

Strange how there was no crushing power in his horrible fingers.

She closed her eyes, sure she was about to die. *What was he waiting for?*

Her door crashed open, and miraculously Johnny was there, the .357 Magnum in his fist. She cried out, and Johnny hit Cole so hard he sank like a deadweight beside her.

Funny, how he didn't look dangerous at all lying there.

"Johnny—" she managed weakly.

Midnight helped her to her feet, brushed his hands along the sides of her cheeks, reassuring himself she was all right before he let her go and ordered her to turn on the light.

Then Johnny knelt beside Cole and felt for his pulse.

"Call the cops. He's out—cold. Get an ambulance. He's only a kid, and I hit him too damned hard."

"He was trying to kill me."

Midnight stared back at her, his black eyes steely. "With what? He was unarmed."

"His hands were around my neck. Johnny, he killed Sam. He was going to kill me, but you got him. You were right to bring us here."

"Was I?" Midnight's voice was curiously dead.

"Yes, the danger's over. Now everything's finally going to be all right. We can live without being afraid. We can get on with our lives."

But Midnight's face was darker and more cynical than ever. "You mean our separate lives?"

Then she realized that he meant there was no longer any reason for them to stay together.

Fourteen

Midnight awoke to the fragile scent of roses clinging to his skin and the cotton sheets—Lacy's scent. Next came the stronger smells of bacon cooking and coffee brewing. He heard the sound of Lacy and Joe singing together in the kitchen and Nero crooning along as well. The morning was so sweet he didn't want to ruin it by dwelling on all the seasons missed, on all the emotions missed.

He didn't want them to leave. This was the golden kind of life he wanted after ten years of loneliness and months of hellish pain. He wanted to make beautiful memories with this woman and their child. He wanted to know all their funny habits, all their dreams. Their lives must become his life. But how?

For a while he lay in bed, snuggled deep inside his cocoon of sheets and covers just listening—enjoying. He knew if he went out there he'd probably break the spell. Then he happened to glance at his watch and saw it was nearly one.

He shot out of bed and opened the blinds to still gray fog—the kind of day that usually depressed him. He snapped them shut. Hell, was it any wonder he'd slept so long and so deeply—nine hours? He was used to nurses and their annoying habit of coming into his room at all hours. Besides he'd been dead with exhaustion from all the excitement. There had been his first game of Russian roulette with a maniac. Cole's break-in, Lacy's near assault, Cole being hauled off on a stretcher by the police and the paramedics. Not to mention the best sex in a decade with a woman Midnight had told himself to despise.

Innocence had warned him to take it easy.

It was a wonder he'd survived.

He dragged on his jeans. He was sore everywhere. But he beamed as he remembered Lacy and the pleasure of her naked body under his, of her hands and mouth on his skin. Just the memory was enough to make him aroused all over again, and he was in that state, pulling on his shirt, when Lacy came to his door, immaculate in a pink blouse and jeans. He knew the memory of their romp in his tangled sheets was just as strong in her because she flushed and drew a quick breath when her eyes darted to the bed and saw he'd just gotten out of it.

He took her flustered expression for a good sign. Her hair was pulled back in a ponytail that made her look younger, that made it easy to remember the first day he'd really met her, the day he'd vowed to have her for his own.

Well, he'd had her, and he wanted her again.

"About last night," he began in a husky, inviting tone so she'd know he was referring to the sex they'd shared and not to Cole.

"I'm sorry," she said wildly. "Sorry that I threw myself at you when you made it plain you didn't really want me. I won't ever do it again."

"Lacy—" he growled.

"Breakfast is ready," she whispered tightly and ran before he could follow his own wild urge to go to her and crush his lips to hers like a hot brand that would make her know she was now his.

Dumb idea. It would take more than sex to keep her. But he wasn't about to let her go.

Alone again and frustrated as hell, he knew it was up to him to come up with a new plan of attack. It had been easy to force her here last night after Cole had pointed that gun between his eyes. But now that that danger was over, he could see she'd take Joe and go—if he didn't figure out a way to stop her.

He could play sick—he damn sure knew how after three months of that stuff—but he'd had enough of the real thing. Besides he didn't want her thinking he was any less of a man than he was. Then he heard Joe talking to Nero in an imaginary kid way, and Midnight knew Joe was the key. Midnight decided to play on her guilt—which, damn her, she should have plenty of. So, he went to the boy, and they had a father-son talk about how to maneuver their woman.

Midnight was whistling the tune they'd been singing earlier when he sat down at the kitchen table with Lacy and Joe. He snapped the newspaper open with a smile and then set it back down and dug into his eggs with such relish that even Lacy smiled for a second before she turned away so he couldn't see.

Joe, who was ignoring his eggs and lavishly spreading his toast with peanut butter and mashed banana, winked at him conspiratorially while Lacy got up for more coffee. "You promised you'd take me to Alcatraz, but Mom wouldn't let me wake you up—" Joe said pretending to sulk, perfecting his act by curling his lip like a corn chip when his mother whirled on him in panic.

"I told you not to mention that, Joe. After yesterday, I'm sure Johnny's tired—"

"I appreciate your concern," Midnight said in a seductive tone and with a smooth look that made her blush. "And I am—a little. And all my big muscles are sore." He smiled lazily. "I was out of practice for so much activity. How about you?"

Lacy, who was leaning over him, setting his coffee cup down with a wobbly hand, flushed to the silver roots of her scalp.

"How about going in a couple of days, Joe?" Midnight finished, keeping his warm gaze glued to Lacy, wondering as he always did if she'd left those top two buttons undone just to stir him.

"That'd be great, Dad!"

Lacy jumped away, so shaken she let go of her coffee cup, which flew to the floor and shattered.

She was sure hell on china.

Midnight pushed back his chair to avoid the spilled coffee pooling beneath his feet.

"You're setting me up deliberately, aren't you, Johnny?"

"It's just coffee," he murmured with pretended innocence, kneeling down and helpfully collecting broken slivers.

"You know that now Cole's in custody, there's no reason for us to stay. The way things are between us would make it impossible."

His voice was crisp. "You could stay if you wanted to."

"It's not that simple."

"It could be. If you'd let it be."

"I want to stay with Johnny, Mom," Joe said, getting up and hugging his father fiercely, as if to shield him from more of her verbal blows. "Don't always be so mean to him."

"What about it, Lacy?" Midnight asked softly. "Joe and I have a lot of catching up to do."

Midnight hugged the boy closer, terrified she'd pick this time to start saying no to Joe.

"You sneak! You know I can't fight Joe. Not about you. Not after you told him— He'd hold it against me forever. Okay! But just for a few days, and . . . just because of Joe."

"Gotcha," Midnight said just as grimly.

"Oh, boy, Mom!"

Joe disentangled his arms from Midnight and went slowly to her. She was so startled and touched when he climbed shyly into her lap and nestled close that she had no idea what to do.

After Joe broke free and ran off with Nero, she sat very still, not even calling him back to remind him he hadn't eaten his eggs. When she dabbed wildly at her eyes with her napkin, Midnight saw the sparkle of tears.

"He doesn't usually hug me. Never before, in fact—" Her soft voice died away.

Midnight got up and went to the sink, so she could savor the wonder of it without knowing he was watching. And he thought: *a few more special moments that are as sweet as that and I'll have her.* And he would have the nights in her bed, too. He was even conceited enough to think it'd be easy. And maybe it would have been, if Colleen hadn't turned up like a dark angel an hour later, just as they were getting ready to go to the nursery like a real family and replace all his houseplants, which had withered while he'd been gone.

The second he saw that carrot red hair and that slim figure squeezed into those skintight black jeans, dread crawled through him. He had hoped he was done with the Douglas family forever.

But when Colleen sprang toward them in that brisk, pushy way of hers, he knew the Douglases weren't through with him after all. Not by a long shot. Midnight's spirits sank even lower when he saw she was carrying an overnight bag.

"Who invited her?" he gritted low, under his teeth, furious at Lacy.

"Be good," was Lacy's tart reply. "I called her. I thought we needed a chaperone."

Maybe it was that remark that set him angrily against Colleen. Maybe it was just because she'd always been big trouble. Maybe it was because she looked like Cole and he felt guilty about Cole. Or maybe it wasn't Colleen at all. Maybe he would have loathed anybody who'd interfered with his need to be with Lacy. Whatever, the dark chill of the gray, foggy day seemed to settle in on him, and his mood took a nosedive.

There was nothing to do but keep his mouth shut and grit his teeth, if Lacy had invited her. So with a false smile he turned on his heel and led the way back to his houseboat. He prayed she'd get bored and leave.

The effort at friendly pretense was so great he leapt for the phone when it rang and was glad it was J.K., home from his honeymoon. His friend invited them to a party the next day, and wanted to know how he and Lacy were, prying a little into his personal life. If Colleen hadn't been there, Midnight might have teased J.K., who'd always been so cold and tough, for finally acting almost human. As it was, Midnight stonily listened to J.K. and warily cocked his other ear to Colleen.

"I got here as fast as I could after I got back from my audition and got your message, Lacy," Colleen was saying. "I can't tell you how relieved I am that they've got Cole, that we can feel safe again. I was terrified he'd come after me."

That rang wrong. Colleen had been demonically fearless. Why the hell did she give a damn about Lacy, anyway? You'd think she'd have a life of her own by now and wouldn't come running the second her stepmother called.

"I haven't checked into a hotel yet."

There was hope.

"No, no. I invited you to stay with us."

Damn. Damn. Damn.

Midnight grimly slammed down the phone and noted the time of J.K.'s party. That was a new habit of his, since the accident, writing down everything. He was in lousy shape, mentally and physically, too lousy to take on the highly energized Colleen. He looked up gloomily. "Sorry about the phone call, Colleen. J.K.'s back from his honeymoon and he wants us to come to a party tomorrow."

"Can Colleen come?" Lacy asked.

Triple damn. "Sure," he replied, his black gaze narrow, his voice cold, hoping Lacy would note he wasn't happy.

Colleen tipped her head back and met his unfriendly gaze with a nervous smile. Colleen's short haircut made her look chillingly like Cole. "It's good to see you too, Johnny," she said, yet he felt some coldness underneath her courtesy.

She knew he didn't want her here, and she didn't give a damn.

A memory flashed. He'd always tried to ignore the troublesome childish crush she'd had on him. She'd come to his room once, and he'd sent her packing.

A woman scorned...

"I'm sorry about your brother," Midnight said in a flat, unemotional tone.

"Why should you be? Lacy told me he nearly shot you."

Again he imagined that coldness in her; it seemed to leap from her to him and coil in his gut, round and round, squeezing tight like a snake. He felt so uneasy, he sprawled back in his chair, trying to hide it. "Yeah, lucky as hell. But there's a poor cabbie lying in the morgue who wasn't."

Colleen paled and fidgeted with her hair.

And he sat up, keener, balancing tensely on the edge of his chair. "You seem ... edgy."

"N-no. I'm just tired from the trip. And worried about Cole."

"That's a switch."

"How is Cole?" Colleen asked.

"Cole is under guard at the hospital," Lacy explained gently, shooting Midnight a warning glare. "They'll be taking him back to the mental institution as soon as he regains consciousness and answers a few questions. Hopefully he'll be able to explain what really happened the night of the fire—why he did what he did. And they want to ask him about Sam."

Colleen went even whiter, and Lacy pressed her hand to comfort her.

"I just hate to think of Cole being locked up again."

Midnight hated the way Colleen hung onto Lacy's hand. "You used to set him up and enjoy it when he got caught instead of you," Midnight persisted, his cool tone biting now.

"I was a child then. It upsets me now."

"Don't tell me you've become the unselfish caring sister in your old age?" Midnight pressed. He was enjoying this. If he was rude enough, maybe she'd leave. "You'll restore my faith in human nature. Few people improve with age."

"Johnny, why are you being so—" Lacy began, furious.

Inside his head he was screaming. *Because I don't want her here. Because after ten damn years of doing without, I want time alone with you and Joe.*

"Oh, it's all right," Colleen replied gently, and her defending him maddened Midnight even more, because it was so fake. "Johnny used to like Cole better than he liked me, and Johnny's been through a lot himself. He's upset. I can understand, because when I think of what Cole's done, what he tried to do... And *I'm* his twin."

Why couldn't Lacy see through her?

"We've talked about it before, Colleen," Lacy said gently. "You're not crazy."

"I want to see him while I'm here," Colleen murmured. "To reassure him that, no matter what he's done, he still has a sister."

"I'm sure that can be arranged," Lacy said.

"No," Midnight thundered.

"Johnny, what is wrong with you this afternoon?" Lacy said.

"I just don't think it's a good idea." He got up and began to pace.

Into this awkward, seething silence, Colleen murmured understandingly, "I'm sure Johnny's right." A pause. "So, now that there's nothing to stop you two from getting on with your lives, do you intend to stay together or separate?"

Midnight shot Colleen a chilling look. "That's none of your damned business."

"We'll be together for a few days," Lacy said. "I'll stay as long as you do. Then I'll start looking for a place of my own."

Lacy's eyes met his. Her message was clear.

If you want to keep Joe and me around—you'd better make her welcome.

"Where will I sleep?" Colleen asked brightly.

"In with me," Lacy said, smiling at Midnight.

And with those three words, she condemned him to hell.

Fifteen

Twenty-four hours of Colleen's saccharine sweetness had made Midnight's nerves as raw as if they'd been flayed with a razor. Twenty-four hours of living with Lacy and not being able to look at her or touch her without Colleen butting in with some brassy little question or cute demand had been unendurable. He'd wanted to show Lacy how gently he could love her. Instead he'd been grumpy as hell. He'd lain in bed all night knowing she was in the next room—with Colleen, their chaperone.

When he'd finally fallen asleep he'd dreamed Lacy was making love to him with her lips and tongue. Then he'd sprung awake, shaking all over, his body hot and hard, his need so strong he'd almost hated Colleen. And he had been even worse to her the next morning, which had made Lacy mad. Thus, Midnight was almost glad to be at J.K.'s rooftop party, even if Lacy was still so upset with him she was avoiding him at the gathering.

And precious time was slipping away.

He stood stiffly beside Honey Cameron and Innocence Lescuer, his face set and grim as he pretended an interest in the painting of Honey's long-lost brother, Raven.

"I would give anything to see Raven again," Honey was saying.

"So when did he disappear?"

"Sometimes it's impossible to resume old relationships that were once precious to you, no matter how you might want to," Midnight said in a bitter voice before he thought, his eyes on Lacy who was talking to one of J.K.'s new lawyers and laughing.

Honey's painful gasp made him realize that he'd inadvertently hurt her. "Sorry," he said more gently. His eyes drifted to Lacy. "I wasn't really talking about your brother."

He left them and scanned the crowd for Colleen, who'd arrived late, tossed him one of those too-bright, triumphant smiles of hers that told him she knew exactly what she was doing. Then she had mysteriously vanished.

Nevertheless, he hated knowing she was anywhere around. It was like she was still that bratty kid he'd baby-sat for, and he knew if he took his eyes off her for a second she'd do something terrible. Baby-sitting her had felt like sitting on a time bomb. Only now, strangely, the feeling was darker and his dread more profound. Which was crazy. She wasn't a child any more.

J.K. handed him a portable phone. "It's the lieutenant in charge of the Douglas case." J.K. touched his arm. "If I can do anything to help—"

Midnight nodded. J.K. had been there for him most of his life. His support meant a hell of a lot.

The lieutenant sounded tense—different. "My men are on their way over there. Until they arrive, you'd better watch your back, pal."

Midnight pressed the phone closer. "What's wrong?"

"Cole Douglas is dying."

Midnight flinched. "I knew I hit him too damned hard—"

"No. *She* did it. A while ago."

"Who?"

"His sister. After she left, he got sick. We think she gave him some sort of injection. It was slow stuff. The doctors are trying to save him, but they don't think they can."

Midnight scanned the crowd frantically. Lacy was still laughing with that lawyer, but Colleen was nowhere in sight.

Neither was Joe.

And then he knew.

The time bomb was about to go off.

As if in slow motion, he looked down and saw an energetic black figure with a cap of carrot red hair shoving Joe into a blue Toyota five stories beneath him.

"Joe!" he screamed.

Colleen slammed the door on the child and then looked up at him and waved gaily as a flock of green parrots flew by. She was smiling but her electric blue gaze was charged with hate.

"Joe!"

Lacy's gaze widened as Midnight rushed toward her and grabbed her hand, bumping a waiter with a tray of champagne glasses as he pulled her wordlessly through the crowd toward the five-story staircase that wound down the center of the mansion to the garage.

Midnight ignored the muted cries behind them. "Where the hell is Colleen taking Joe?" he demanded.

"To Alcatraz. They were both bored at the party. I thought it'd be all right. I thought it would save you having to—"

He pulled her down the stairs.

"Johnny, what's wrong?"

"*It was her—Colleen.* All the time it was her. Not Cole. Not Sam. I've had a feeling ever since I hit Cole that something wasn't right, and when Colleen came the feeling got worse. I should have trusted my instincts. She murdered her own mother, our fathers, Sam—everybody. She tried to kill Cole a few minutes ago. She'll be merciless to Joe.''

"I thought it was Cole's voice that night in Vienna."

"She's an actress. She could always mimic anybody."

They plunged into the darkened garage and he jumped into J.K.'s black sports car. He grabbed the keys from under the floorboard and jammed them into the ignition. He punched the automatic door opener.

Then he turned to her. "Tell the police and J.K. where I've gone. There's a phone in the car, so I'll call you and tell you where—"

She opened the passenger door. "I'm going with you."

"Damn it! No!"

He was backing out as she jumped in.

"Lacy—" he thundered, braking hard.

"Johnny, you may need me."

"Because you think I'm inadequate?"

"No...I have to prove to you—that I'm no longer the girl who left you for Sam, for whatever reason. I have to make you know that I really do love you, that I've always loved you, that no matter how terrible the danger is to you and Joe, it's mine, too."

"Get out. The last thing I want is for you to be hurt proving some idiotic point."

"Johnny Midnight, you're not the only one who needs to prove to himself he's a hero."

And then he knew that the long years had been as hellishly empty for her as they'd been for him. His black eyes struck hers and he felt a strange new tenderness. A new forgiveness. He would have given anything to dwell on this sudden sweetness he felt for her, but there was no time. His hand slid carelessly over her face ever so briefly.

Then his hands gripped the steering wheel with grim determination and the car shot out of the garage like a bullet.

Midnight caught the blue Toyota on the Golden Gate Bridge and tailgated closely. Joe, unaware of the danger, waved gaily. An odd unaccountable fear quickened in Midnight when Colleen veered off the freeway and took the coast road to Tam Junction, but he followed right behind her anyway.

He remembered almost nothing about his accident, but the minute she chose that road he knew he would have given anything to have avoided it.

The highway climbed through eucalyptus trees. The curves were too tight for the Toyota. They were easier for J.K.'s car.

Not so easy for Midnight though. The strange, darkly pulsing panic inside him worsened when they broke out into brown windswept hills with sheer cliffs crumbling to a rocky shore.

They were approaching a curve.

The curve.

How the hell had she known when he hadn't known till now?

In a blinding flash Midnight saw the yellow oncoming car, and then the van in his lane that was passing it, and the blue one behind him, tailing too close, hemming him in. He remembered veering into the rusty guardrail, and how the blue car had rammed him from behind.

Deliberately.

He'd flown free of the wreckage and seen a woman in black smiling down at his wrecked car.

Colleen.

"Johnny, watch out!" Lacy screamed. "She turned around and she's coming straight at us."

Midnight hadn't realized that he'd taken his foot off the accelerator, that the Toyota had charged ahead of him, made a sharp U-turn and was speeding head-on toward them in their lane.

Lacy screamed and covered her eyes.

At the last second, Midnight spun the wheel to the left and gunned it.

There was no one in the oncoming lane. He missed the guardrail by an inch. Tires squealing, he made a U-turn and raced down the mountain after the speeding Toyota.

Lacy's terrified eyes locked with his. "She wants to kill us all."

"She did me a favor back there, Lacy," he said slowly. "Now I remember why I fought so hard to live."

"Why?"

God, he'd been such a fool, but there was no time to tell her. No time to beg her to forgive him.

He took one hand off the wheel and reached for her. He fitted his fingers through hers in the old way. Their way.

And his touch and his eyes sent the message of his timeless soul-deep love.

He had come back for her.

All the pain and the terror had been for her.

He hoped they both lived so he could tell her properly.

When Midnight loped onto his dock, Colleen was sitting in a lawn chair on the deck of the houseboat, her .38 tucked neatly in the fold of a paperback book as she waited for him.

"Where's Joe?" Midnight demanded, scared she'd already killed him.

"Inside—tied up for the moment," Colleen whispered. "We're going on a little cruise. Won't you join us? And go back and get Lacy. The party wouldn't be complete without the Douglas number-one party girl."

"You're crazy."

"Special," came the deadly whisper. "Or consider me someone who's chosen an alternate life-style. Oh, and, hey, congratulations! You were good on the Stinson road today. I didn't think you had a chance in hell. Too bad for you though—it's always better to die fast than slow. And you'd have taken me out, too. I'm going to get away now."

Rage consumed him as Midnight started toward her.

Her whisper was like steel. "I said get Lacy."

He stared into her crazily lit blue eyes.

"Or Joe dies now."

Midnight held up his hand, and Lacy who'd been waiting by the car for his signal came running.

To her death.

No, dear God, she couldn't die.

He hoped she'd called the cops, as he'd told her to.

Then they were on board, and he was terrified for all their lives.

The engines were running. A small runabout with an outboard was tied off the stern.

"Cast off," Colleen ordered almost jauntily.

She was a monster.

There was nothing to do but grimly obey her.

When they reached the bay, Colleen commanded him to head for the Golden Gate Bridge. A cold wind had been freshening all day, and the sea was rough. The bulky houseboat slid clumsily up and down the large waves.

"She's designed for smooth water, not the Pacific," Midnight ground out. "She'll break up."

Colleen smiled. "I hope so." She studied the instruments and gave him a bearing. "Set the automatic pilot and get down inside. Now! Both of you!"

She followed close behind them with the gun. Joe was blindfolded and gagged and tied to a chair in the living room. When Lacy started toward him, Colleen waved her away with her gun. Nero could be heard snarling and growling from behind Joe's bedroom door.

There was an album and a rusty lighter and a camera on the coffee table. Two half-filled glasses of cola sparkled invitingly. "Sit down," Colleen said. "Have a cola. No, first, take a look at the album. Enjoy. We—or rather *you*—don't have much time."

The houseboat was pitching crazily, groaning. Midnight
flipped through the album, stalling. Because of the boat's
movement, he got queasy just looking at the thing.

It was all there—the bright, glamorous facade of the
Douglases' life and the darker side, too. They'd had it all—
fame, glory, wealth and power, but on the dark side, they
had been so emotionally stunted they hadn't known how to
nurture one another. They hadn't known how to love, how
to cherish. In the end, they had destroyed everyone they
touched, even themselves, and they had stunted the soul of
their neglected daughter.

Colleen was smiling proudly as he studied the pictures,
when he glanced up at her. She looked like a girl, almost
happy, with a short lock of red hair falling across her
smooth brow.

"Why?" Midnight's hand had frozen on the page of the
bagged bodies being lifted into the ambulance. "How?"

Her blue eyes shone with fierce pride, and he saw that the
actress in her wanted center stage. She wanted to brag about
everything.

"It was my fault they quarreled that night at the warehouse. I sent Daddy one of those pictures Cole took of her
and her lover—to make her suffer and to blackmail him.
One minute Daddy was picking paint colors and telling her
how to arrange her papier-mâché columns around the
bandstand. The next he was waving that picture and screaming. Then he stormed out in a rage.

"Mother said she was going to leave Daddy and put us in
a horrible boarding school. She laughed when I begged her
not to, and I knew she had to die.

"Cole and I had been playing cards with your father, and
I had stolen his lighter. We followed Daddy downstairs to
plead with him not to send us away, but he told us he was
through with us all.

"I saw the piles of garbage and paint thinner on the bottom floor. Cole went outside, and I got the idea. It was easy

to pour the paint thinner and set the fires. You wouldn't believe how easy and how fast. When the flames roared up the rafters, I just wished I had enough paint thinner to burn up the whole world. Then your father came tearing down those stairs with his hair and clothes on fire. When he looked into my eyes, I laughed."

"You're a monster."

"He knew I did it, and I was terrified he was going to kill me. But he fell down at my feet. And then Daddy came back and put the lighter in Abe's hand.

"I made Daddy think Cole set the fire. Cole was so numb and felt so bad because he had taken the picture of Mother he didn't say much. But he felt worse later when I told him he was as bad as me because he was my twin. He kept screaming he wasn't, and he had that breakdown. Which was wonderful because that meant I could blackmail Daddy for years and years, and he thought it was Cole. I killed Daddy when Cole escaped, so Cole would be blamed. Cole only came to you—to warn you—about me."

"Oh, my God," Lacy said, sobbing, sinking in a chair beside Joe. "All these years I thought you were my friend. I—I can't believe—"

"The night my father died he regained consciousness just long enough to say the name Douglas," Midnight said. "I thought he meant Sam."

"When you came to our Christmas party that night and accused Daddy, you scared me out of my mind. You looked at me like you could see through me. You shouldn't have pushed."

"There's no need for you to kill anybody else," Midnight said very softly. "You can't get away with it."

"Oh, but there is a need and I will get away with it. I've gotten away with everything else. And every story needs an ending—the last clipping. I like doing things that make the papers. Maybe I'm like my father after all. I'm going to sink this barge underneath the Golden Gate Bridge with all of you on board, and I'll just motor away. I have the money I got from Daddy, a phony passport—everything I need to start over."

"How could you pretend you loved me," Lacy cried. "And Joe, too?"

"Let them go," Midnight said. "Kill me. Sink my houseboat, but let them go. You'll have your clipping—"

"You wretched fool! I hate her more than anybody. When she came, she took everything I ever wanted. Everybody admired her—Daddy, Grandmother. The newspaper people thought she was wonderful. You loved her, too. I was invisible when she was around. Nobody ever loved me, and because they didn't, they all paid. And now you're going to pay, too."

They were under the Golden Gate Bridge. The houseboat was pitching crazily when Lacy sprang at Colleen's throat, but Colleen was quicker, deadlier, faster. Before Midnight could react she'd struck Lacy with the butt of her gun, and Lacy had crumpled to the floor. Colleen would have hit her again, but Midnight had hurled himself forward and she turned the gun on Joe.

"Do you feel lucky enough to chance another round of Russian roulette?" Colleen whispered, smiling cruelly.

"Not with Joe's life," Midnight snarled.

"Good. I want you to open the sea cocks in the heads, underneath the sink, the shower... And, oh, there's one that has something to do with the water that cools the engine."

"I know where they are!"

"Then open them, damn it!"

She held the gun on him while he did what she'd ordered. She shot several holes through the floor.

Water was pouring inside the boat when they returned to the living room and discovered both Lacy and Joe were gone.

"Where the hell are they—" Terrified, Colleen wildly pointed her gun at Midnight. "Nighty night—" She was about to pull the trigger when Lacy answered her.

"I'm right here, Colleen," came a cool voice from behind them.

Colleen whirled on Lacy, pulling the trigger. Lacy fired Midnight's .357 Magnum at the same moment.

Colleen staggered backward, shot through the fleshy part of the shoulder. Lunging for the hand that held the gun, Midnight went down on top of her. They rolled over together. She punched him in the ribs, and he writhed in agony. Somehow he held on.

Then her gun went off again.

Joe and Nero leapt into the room.

Lacy screamed in terror.

There was a terrible stillness. Then an agonized male groan.

"Johnny," Lacy whispered, sinking to her knees, crawling toward him. "Johnny— Please get up. Johnny!"

"I'm okay," he said, pushing himself up, breathing hard, holding his side, trying to grin, but only managing a grimace. He had Colleen's gun. Blood from Colleen's wound was pooling on the carpet.

"Let's get the hell off this barge before she goes down." He yanked Colleen to her feet. "Joe get the album and the lighter. When the police finish with it, maybe they'll let her keep a couple of precious pictures to enjoy while she rots in prison or in some mental institution.

"No..." Colleen whispered.

Midnight grabbed a flare gun. Then they all scrambled out on deck. The gusting wind felt like blasts of wet ice. Colleen began to fight him. His hand slipped as he was forcing her over the side into the runabout. She screamed once, kicked off from the houseboat with her feet and dove into the icy waves.

Deliberately.

They watched for her a long time, but she didn't come up.

The houseboat was listing as Midnight helped Lacy and Joe and Nero into the runabout. Midnight got in and cut the line, and as they drifted away he shot off two flares.

Five motorboats were speeding toward them. He ignored them all and folded Lacy and Joe into his arms and held on to them tightly and even grabbed for Nero when he whined jealously.

A minute or two was as long as Joe could ever hug anybody except maybe his dog—especially when Johnny's houseboat was sinking and five motorboats were bouncing over the waves to save them.

"Why don't you kiss him, Mom? I won't look. Why don't you tell him you'll marry him too?"

"Because he hasn't asked me yet."

Midnight laced his fingers through hers and gripped her tightly, staring into her eyes and thinking how unbearably precious she was to him. "The only reason I'm alive is because of you. Right before my car went over that cliff, I saw your face. Your love shone through my fear, through the blindness of my fury, through the long dark hours of pain at the hospital. Lacy, I hurt you terribly. I blame myself for everything that happened."

"Don't."

"The only reason I wanted to live was to come back to you. I was wrong to hate you for Sam. I drove you to him. I abandoned you—pregnant with my child. I hated you unfairly for years. I'm not asking you to forgive me," he said tenderly. "I'm begging you."

Lacy's eyes shone with love; her face had grown radiant.

And Joe dutifully covered his eyes, thinking they would kiss.

Instead Lacy touched Midnight's face, murmuring, "The hurtful years are over. All that will ever matter is that you came back to me."

"You and Joe are my reasons for living."

"As you will always be ours."

"Marry me," he said.

"I love you," Joe heard them both whisper at the same moment right before their lips came together eagerly and he hid his eyes again.

But he felt so warm and tingly he cheated and peeked through his fingers as they kissed. And the kiss went on and on—longer than the most awfulest, mushiest hug.

It seemed like the awfulest eternity before his mother finally caught her breath and said, "Yes."

Epilogue

San Francisco was wrapped in lavender twilight as Midnight slammed the door of his car after a long day of work and walked up the steps to his sprawling white house in Twin Peaks. The two-story affair that topped the hill wasn't a castle, and he damn sure wasn't a prince. But Lacy had said her life with him was better and truer than any fairy tale. She was talented when it came to turning a house into a home, talented at making him love her more with the passing of each day.

It had been nine months since his accident, nine months since Lacy had come back into his life. Six months of marriage and near-idyllic happiness. Not that Lacy and he had begun as most couples. They already had a nine-year-old son who could now sometimes endure being hugged for as long as five minutes, who'd been to Alcatraz at least half a dozen times. And Cole had survived, and was living nearby.

A life filled with love was a glorious life. Midnight knew because he'd done without it so long.

He set his briefcase down and pushed open his front door, expecting Lacy to be there. Because every night she seemed to know the exact moment he would come to her.

Instead he heard Mario's drums and a thundered, *"Surprise."*

J.K. was there along with a heavily pregnant Honey and Heather and everyone else they knew, even Amelia and Innocence Lescuer. But it was Lacy he saw, beautiful and radiantly pregnant herself, though as yet nobody but he knew. It was Lacy he heard whispering above all the other, "Surprise."

It was Lacy's slim body he felt melting against him, her breasts fuller, her skin smelling sweetly of sunshine and roses as he folded her into his arms. And there was warmth and laughter and clapping all around them as he crushed her to him, his strong hands like bands of iron, in a fiercely possessive embrace.

"What's the occasion?" Midnight asked hoarsely.

"You are. Officially though, it's our six-month anniversary."

"Every day I celebrate that," he murmured huskily against her ear.

"And every night," she whispered back to him. "We're going to fill this house with happiness and our children."

At that thought, he flushed with dark passion and forgot for a second or two that they were the center of attention. He kissed her deeply, thoroughly, his open mouth so wet and searing, she began to tremble.

And as he held her tighter than ever, the room seemed to fill with a glorious fiery light. It seemed to him they were in a roaring tunnel with wind and heat rushing past them at an exhilarating speed.

He had fought his way back from the gates of hell to find her.

Heaven was her smile. Her lips on his. Her voice when she sang to him. His child growing inside her. Heaven was their life together—their love.

Heaven was Lacy in his arms, and he intended to keep her there forever.

* * * * *

*Watch for WILD INNOCENCE,
the third book in Ann Major's
SOMETHING WILD series,
coming in February 1994!*

SILHOUETTE® Desire®

It's the men you've come to know and love... with a bold, new look that's going to make you take notice!

MAN of the MONTH 1994

January: *SECRET AGENT MAN* by Diana Palmer
February: *WILD INNOCENCE* by Ann Major (second title in her SOMETHING WILD miniseries)
March: *WRANGLER'S LADY* by Jackie Merritt
April: *BEWITCHED* by Jennifer Greene
May: *LUCY and THE STONE* by Dixie Browning
June: *HAVEN'S CALL* by Robin Elliott

And that's just the first six months!
Later in the year, look for books by Barbara Boswell, Cait London, Joan Hohl, Annette Broadrick and LassSmall....

MAN OF THE MONTH
ONLY FROM
SIILHOUETTE DESIRE

MOMNEW